WOLF 359

EDWARD J BRINK

ISBN: 0692661573
ISBN 13: 9780692661574

THE YEAR 2324

A small desk lamp illuminates the darkened interior of the Oval Office as the President of the United Nations sits at his desk reading a long memo. Frowning down at the document he takes off his glasses and rubs his eyes tiredly. The world has grown too much for one man. In fact, it was now technically, worlds. As if it wasn't hard enough to lead one planet, there were now thirty-two major and minor planetary colonies, the hundreds of local governments on those planets, fifty space stations both official and fringe, interplanetary trade, territorial and resource disputes and the five hundred or so political, terrorist and non-governmental groups both supporting and opposing pretty much every issue and idea you could think of. The large grandfather clock in the corner of the room suddenly tolls midnight snapping the President out of his reverie.

Glancing up at the clock, he tries to overcome the exhaustion dimming his wits, 'Used to be able to work until three or four without any problem,' he thinks to himself with a sigh, 'You would think they would have come up with some sort of anti-aging pill by now.' Standing up slowly, the President walks over to the small bar located in the corner of the office and pours himself a small glass of scotch. Raising the glass to his lips he suddenly finds himself looking at one of the many pictures lining the wall on this side of the room. It is an old college picture of himself standing with a young man. 'Ravanna,' he thinks to himself nostalgically as he downs the rest of his drink in a toast to his old friend. Suddenly a loud knock emanates from the door. Turning around tiredly he sees the Secretary of Defense rush in, his face tense, 'Mr. President, there's been an invasion.'

The President looks at him sharply, 'Alpha Centauri?'

'Yes sir,' the man says as he walks over to the bar and pours himself a drink, 'Sirius must be getting desperate after that last round of sanctions.'

'What war hasn't been an act of desperation?' The President asks quietly as he turns to the window and tries to hide a shudder of dismay. Staring out into the darkened grounds of the White House he feels a wave of dread pass over him gently.

The twin suns of Alpha Centauri rise high into the beautiful blue of the early morning sky as eighteen-year-old Private

Robert Renault stands aboard a landing ship as they debark from one of the mammoth carriers stationed in the upper atmosphere of the planetary colony. Crammed into the hold around him are the hundred men and boys of H Company, 3rd Infantry Division, outfitted in their brand new green and grey high tech assault kits. Looking around at the familiar faces of his platoon Robert notices that the experienced men of the company chat idly or peer out the landing ship's portholes, the new recruits nervously recheck all of their equipment and weapons, their hands slightly shaking from a mixture of excitement and fear but the old timers, the real veterans, look on edge, a quiet mix of alert presence and the cold dread rising from their bellies. Robert realizes that it must be the new equipment that is setting them on edge. The greatest combat indicator is always how well supplied you are by the higher ups. Gulping down his own apprehension, Robert reaches into his pants pocket, closes his eyes shut in concentration and begins fingering the beads of his rosary. 'Dear Lord, please protect the men of my company on this day. Please keep all of us safe as we prepare to go into battle. If you do see it fit for someone to get hurt please let it be me, just keep everyone else out of harm's way. But most of all take care of Valentine. She is the most important person in my life. Whatever happens make sure that she is taken care of,' opening his eyes Robert glances around, feeling almost refreshed, before pulling his hand out of his pocket and doing a quick sign of the cross, 'Amen.' A distant explosion suddenly rocks the air and makes the landing ship shudder.

'What the hell was that?' someone calls out.

Frowning, Robert makes his way over to one of the portholes and pushes his way through the crowded soldiers. Peering out the window all he can see are the baby blue skies and the white clouds of the Alpha Centauri morning. Suddenly he catches a glint of light in the distance. Squinting his eyes against the early morning sun he sees something coming at them so fast it creates a wake among the white clouds.

'Incoming!' someone yells as the men around him try to take cover but Robert stares forward in rapt fascination, unable to move as the streaking missile comes right for him. The landing craft's alarm klaxon goes off and the ship begins firing silver and white flares into the air in order to disorient the missiles locking system. The missile suddenly loses the lock and veers away from them but then it crashes into the carrier above them in a massive fireball. All Robert can do is watch in stunned horror as hundreds of soldiers that were inside fall out of the gaping hole toward the ground thousands of feet below.

Fleet Admiral Ward strides into the darkened state room of the space carrier Hermes and finds a shadowy figure standing at the observation window staring down at the planet Alpha Centauri below. 'They took the bait sir, all fast attack aircraft have moved to intercept the landing force,' Ward says as he stops and stands at attention from a respectful distance.

The shadowy figure turns his head fractionally in the direction of Ward, 'Good, and the ground element's attack through the front lines?'

'They are making good progress,' Ward says as he frowns at the other man, 'The landing by the airborne element behind the lines has caused a lot of confusion and blocked reinforcements.'

'Excellent, the enemy will be so preoccupied with the armored spearheads pushing through their frontline and the airborne landing in their rear that they won't see the real objective of our attack until it's too late.'

'I'll pass along your orders to begin the strike,' Ward says as he turns to go but then the other man raises a restraining hand.

'That won't be necessary Admiral,' he says in a carefully modulated voice.

Ward frowns in confusion, 'Sir?'

'Tell the men, Ravanna will be personally leading this one.'

'Are you sure command and control can spare you sir?' Ward asks apprehensively.

'Yes,' the shadowy figure says as he finally turns and heads for the door, 'there's something I want to see for myself.'

A torrent of incoming rounds explode all around Robert and his company as they sprint out of their landing ship and dive for cover. Robert takes cover in an impact crater and looks around in fear as the men call for targets and shout orders above the din and furor of the raging battle. Peering over the rim of the crater he can see small flashes from enemy weapons up on their objective, the massive hill overlooking the landing troops. Several of his squad mates rush forward and take cover in a crater as rounds zip by but one of them steps on the pressure plate of a mine and it explodes tossing them all into the air like rag dolls. His heart beating hard with fear, Robert glances back in panic and suddenly see's the company commander, Captain George James, calmly walking up through the incoming fire. Around him his adjutants, forward observers and radio men crouch and cower in fear but oddly enough he just seems to consider the bullets and mini rounds coming in as more of an inconvenience. He turns to his adjutant in annoyance, 'Lieutenant why the hell are they all taking cover?'

'Hey get moving 2nd Platoon!' the Lieutenant yells out to the men as he runs forward but an incoming round knocks him to the ground.

Captain James presses a hand to his headset radio, 'Alpha Six, this is Bravo One. Successful infil at target. Light enemy contact so far. Moving to Objective. Out.'

Turning angrily, he sees Robert taking cover, a look of terror on his face, 'Private, come on, get up and push up,' he says as he kicks him in the rear and then moves on to the other soldiers taking cover.

Above the landing soldiers, on the hill overlooking the battlefield a sniper hidden inside a small bunker aims through a magnified scope at the small men running around like ants below. With a deep, calming breath he fills his lungs and steadies his scope on one of the enemy soldiers moving up.

Robert breathes hard as he puts one foot in front of the other. His ears ring with the concussion of incoming artillery and the snap and zip of rounds being fired by a hidden machine gun somewhere on the hill above. Suddenly something smacks him hard in the chest and Robert gets knocked backward onto the ground.

The sniper watches as his target gets knocked down head over heels and then takes aim at another man. Gently pulling the trigger, the rifle recoils and he watches him fall too. Looking over at the machine gun crew he points at a group moving up on the right. They nod and adjust their fire but then the sniper hears something. Like a mechanical groan slowly growing in power and force. Suddenly the sniper's face grows tense with understanding.

Robert tries to breath but with every breathe it becomes harder. 'Chest cavity is filling with air,' he suddenly realizes with a sinking feeling. Pushing down the fear rising up from within, he abruptly remembers Valentine. Then with a sudden concussion the hill above erupts in a massive explosion. 'Valentine,' he thinks, as he tries to remember the beautiful blue eyes and bright smile of his love.

James watches the flowering explosion in grim fascination for a moment before pressing his headset, 'Alpha Six, this is Bravo One. Enemy contact at grid Four Quebec eliminated. Thirty casualties Priority T1, Fourteen casualties Priority T4. Waiting for link up with Task Force Armor.'

'Roger,' the voice in his headset responds calmly, 'Special Operations Command will take it from here.'

A black transport ship suddenly swoops down through the clouds and silently lands at the top of the hill while above them, rising into the smoke filled morning sky, looms a massive mushroom cloud from the explosion. A group of ten men kitted in dark battle dress uniforms quickly jump out of the craft and immediately begin to move toward the bunkers lining the ridge at the top of the hill.

The ground team makes it to the entrance of the command bunker and halt on both sides. One man, his code name "RAVANNA" stenciled on his back, pulls a black fiber optic cable from the side of his helmet and pokes it around the corner. Using a small flip down eye piece he looks through the fiber optic for any movement but all is completely still. He pauses for a moment to make sure before finally pressing a button on his wrist command console. The nine other men instantly file into the structure keeping close to one another and covering every angle. Ravanna goes in last and watches as the team move as one to a staircase leading downward into the heart of the hill. The team reaches the bottom of the first

set of stairs before they silently come to a halt. Ravanna noise-
lessly moves down past them, his sound dampening boots al-
lowing him to move like a ghost. He reaches the bottom of the
stairs and once again pokes his fiber optic around the corner.
Looking through his eye piece he immediately sees a light go
out underneath one of the hallway doors. He quickly presses a
series of buttons on his wrist, his hand slightly shaking from
the adrenaline pumping through his system. Behind him he
can feel the men of his team suddenly tense in anticipation. A
counter begins in his ear piece, 'Three, two, one.'

Instantly one man falls to the ground around the corner,
his small, black submachine gun covering the team as they
move to the opposite wall and cover the now darkened door.
Code name Ravanna moves up once again, his heart now
pounding as he silently walks to the doorway. He pauses at
the wall next to the door as two of his men join him. The rest
hang back and wait. Ravanna pushes another button on his
wrist command console and the man behind him gives the
door a quick swipe with a small handheld scanner. Ravanna
hears the all clear signal in his ear piece. Blinking away the
sweat beading on his forehead he quickly places a small detonator on the door before beginning the counter, 'Three, two,
one.'

The door is blown off its hinges in a flash of light and
smoke. Ravanna immediately enters but then a man rises up
out of the smoke ahead, his body silhouetted perfectly against
the light shining from a computer screen. Without a moment's

hesitation Ravanna immediately fires an inaudible burst from his submachine gun and the man drops to the ground. His heart in his throat, Ravanna clears forward carefully while the rest of the team file in and clear behind him. He presses a hand to his head set, 'This is Ravanna. Enemy HQ neutralized.' Walking up to the man, he bends down to take a closer look at his face. But as he peers through the low light gloom he suddenly feels his stomach go cold. Quietly hemorrhaging blood from his mouth that shines in the light of the computer is an exact replica of himself, a clone.

CHAPTER 1

THE MAN ON A MISSION

The last rays of the sun gleam over the horizon as a light rain drizzles down onto the deck of the aircraft carrier U.N.S. Fallujah. Lieutenant Commander Aaron Chandler glances down nervously at his watch as the plane lift slowly raises him from the mechanical bowels of the ship's interior into the cold greyness of the North Atlantic. He places a microphone headset over his U.N. beret, plugs it into his personal role radio and then looks up as the lift shudders to a halt. 'Control, what is E.T.A.?' Chandler asks into his mic.

'10 seconds', a woman's voice announces over his headset. Chandler steps out onto the deck and turns to his right just as a hybrid Space, Air, Sea shuttle bearing the insignia of the United Nations roars overhead. A look of curiosity slowly spreads across the young commander's tanned face as he watches the ship turn and then land nearby. As a commander in the United Nation's navy he was used to the privileges of rank but this was a situation which he had no idea how to handle. For some reason the President of the United Nations had requested to meet with him. Although the man was an old college buddy of his father Chandler still could not wrap his head around this situation. Taking a deep breath, he reassuringly touches his holstered pistol as the shuttle's ramp drops and the President of the United Nations debarks. They walk toward each other smiling and shake hands vigorously. 'My god Aaron, how long has it been?' The President asks.

'It's been 10 years Mr. President,' Chandler says.

'Yes, that sounds about right,' the President says as an inflection of pain enters his voice, 'I miss your father greatly; he was my truest friend through all our years together. But I especially miss him at times like these. In fact, that's why I've come for you.'

Chandler gives him an inquisitive look, 'Sir?'

The President looks to the pilot of the shuttle and motions for him to prepare for takeoff. He looks back to Chandler. 'Come on, there's not a moment to lose. I'll brief you on the way.'

Rain begins to splatter against the viewports of the shuttle as the President and Chandler sit next to each other in the dark green, metallic hold. The President stretches his legs out in front of him and then pulls out an old fashioned Winslow pipe. As he places a pinch of tobacco in the bowl he glances over at the younger man, 'Just give me a second here Commander. I can think a little clearer with a smoke.'

Chandler fidgets uncomfortably in his seat, 'So what exactly did you need me for sir?'

The President ignores him as he lights the pipe and then pulls on it until the bowl glows red in the dim light of the cabin. He exhales a cloud of smoke as he turns to Chandler, 'Now then. In order for you to help me we need to establish the facts, how familiar are you with the Sirian invasion of Alpha Centauri?' the President asks as the shuttle shudders from a wind gust.

Chandler narrows his eyes, 'That was that invasion by those rebels right?'

The President gives him an approving look, 'That's correct. Fifteen years ago they were wiped out by Special Operations Command when they tried to take over Alpha Centauri. SOC leader at the time went by code name Ravanna. It was a brilliantly planned campaign that brought peace to the inner systems but something happened during that war. For some reason code name Ravanna just went off the grid when the conflict ended,' the President adds solemnly before continuing, 'It's now been more than four years since his whole taskforce disappeared into the unknown regions of space.'

'What happened to them?' Chandler asks, his interest now piqued.

'No one knows for sure,' the President says in a distant voice as he thoughtfully puffs on his pipe. Chandler sits in silent contemplation for a moment as he tries to imagine what could have caused those men to want to disappear like that. The President leans toward him, 'So then I guess you might be wondering how you fit into all of this?'

'Yes sir,' Chandler says keenly as he looks at the President.

'I contacted you because I need someone I can trust by my side,' the President says as he sets down the pipe and leans in, his face now very serious. Chandler nods gravely as he looks at the older man. The President takes a deep breath and sighs. 'To sum it up, everything's gone to hell,' he says as he looks away, his face a mixture of bitterness and frustration. 'We've been getting strange reports coming in from the colony worlds. There's something big stirring out there. Nothing definitive but I have reason to believe that it is somehow connected with the disappearance of code name Ravanna.'

'What sort of reports?' Chandler asks as he starts to realize the magnitude of the situation that he has been so suddenly swept up into.

'My sources say we have infiltrators in the command structure,' the President says as he rubs his eyes tiredly.

Chandler frowns in concentration, 'So you think Ravanna has come back and has been infiltrating the UN command? But why?'

'I'm not sure,' the President says almost forlornly, 'but I should warn you that after the war ended he was a volunteer as part of the biological warfare project.'

'What enhancements did he receive?' Chandler asks in alarm, his skin crawling at the prospect of facing what many considered to be non-human soldiers.

Suddenly the President presses a hand to his ear and for the first time Chandler notices that he is wearing a miniature ear piece, barely visible to the eye. Chandler watches him as he listens to the report coming in but then the President's face suddenly goes pale as he turns to him, 'We just received a report saying that Ravanna has just turned himself in.'

Chandler raises an eyebrow, 'Where? One of the colony worlds?'

'No,' the President says as he looks at him thoughtfully, 'he's here on Earth.'

A now steady sheet of rain beats down on the hard, grey concrete of the Costa Verde maximum security prison facility as the shuttle lands with a jolt. Chandler leads the way down the ramp and looks up through the rain at the towering, floodlit facility but then he spots a man in a white lab coat trotting toward them. The man, small, gray haired and in his fifties, walks up out of the rain but as he wipes the water from his face Chandler notices that he is shaking slightly. He notices Chandler eyeing him and smiles nervously. The President comes down and stands next to Chandler, 'Tillman', the President says with a nod.

Tillman anxiously cleans the condensation from his glasses and puts them back on, 'Mr. President, we weren't told you were coming but I assure you that everything is under control. We just need a little more time to assess the...'

The President suddenly cuts him off, 'Take me to him now,' he says grimly.

Tillman looks at the President through his heavy lidded eyes before nodding slowly and pressing a hand to his headset, 'We're coming in,' he says before turning and walking off toward the facility.

Holding his hand up Tillman leads the President and Chandler through a brightly lit hallway as they pass through one sealed blast door after another, 'As you can see, this facility has been specifically designed to keep the prisoner from escaping. Every door has a biometric scanner that only I can access.' They finally come to a giant sealed blast door. Tillman swipes his security clearance card but as the door slowly grinds open Chandler's headset suddenly starts to screech wildly. He quickly yanks it off, his face contorted in agony.

The President turns to him in concern, 'You okay Aaron?'

He nods and lifts a hand reassuringly, 'Yes sir, I just need a minute.'

The President looks at Tillman but he smiles, 'Ravanna can remotely hack into any network so we've had the storage unit specially designed to interfere with any signal transmissions,' he looks down at Chandler, 'What you felt now is what he feels at all times'.

'Not sure if that's a good thing,' Chandler grumbles as he turns off the radio and places the headset back on. The giant blast door finally grinds to a halt and the three of them turn to stare into a huge empty storage hangar with no lights. Further back, on the far side of the hangar they perceive a small metal container with a narrow observation slit running along the side. The President strides confidently into the hangar but Chandler grabs his shoulder, 'We should stop here sir.' Together they stare intently at the container but the observation slit running along the side of it is too darkened for them to see anything.

'Why's it so dark Danny?' the President asks, turning toward the scientist.

'We find that it helps to keep him calm,' Tillman answers but the President notices that he has a queer gleam in his eye as he stares at the container.

'So who exactly is he?' Chandler asks.

The President opens his mouth to answer but his voice is suddenly drowned out by a long hollow boom that resonates from the container in front of them. They all turn and stare at the container but then a pair of red eyes light up the observation slit. The President strains his eyes to try and get a better look but only the glowing eyes can be perceived as it keenly observes them. Suddenly the eyes narrow into slits and then a furious cacophony of booms resonate out into the hangar as the being within tries to break out. Chandler grabs the President's arm, 'We need to leave sir.'

The President stares spellbound at the container, 'What?'

'Now sir!' Chandler yells, pulling the President's arm.

The President suddenly snaps out of his reverie and begins following Chandler but then he turns back to Tillman, 'Destroy him', he says, both anger and fear contorting his features.

Tillman's eyes darken, 'But I don't have the authorization to access the containment unit.'

The President turns in exasperation and looks at him, 'Now you do,' he says gruffly as he pulls out his own personal access card and hands it to him.

Back in the brightly lit hallway the President and Chandler quickly walk back to the shuttle. Chandler switches back on his headset and turns to the President, 'Isn't code name Ravanna a prisoner of war if not a deserter who should be brought up on charges? Since when do we carry out summary executions like this?'

'This isn't the time for these questions Aaron,' the President says as he walks.

Chandler suddenly stops, 'But why sir? He is obviously contained. What's the real reason you brought me here?'

The President stops and stares hard at him, 'I told you why. It is my duty as President to keep a small problem like this from becoming a larger problem that could put a lot of people at risk.'

Tillman walks up to the now quiet container with the President's access card in hand. He peers through the observation slit but can't see anything inside. He walks over to the other side of the container and attaches the card to the container's built in conduit. He takes a step back and looks at the container with anticipation. Suddenly his eyes widen with fear as he hears a low rasping breathing coming from the container. 'Did it work?' an insidious voice quietly asks from the darkness of the container.

Tillman falls to a knee and stammers, 'Yes, Ravanna.'

Chandler and the President finally reach the entrance to the facility but then the President stops and looks at Chandler, 'I don't want you to worry Aaron,' he says in a conciliatory voice, 'But you're going to have to trust me on this one. He was once a man that deserved respect and due process but with the bio enhancements he is simply too dangerous. The world is now a safer place.' Suddenly the lights go out overhead.

The President looks around in concern but Chandler just presses his hand to his headset, 'Get the Q.R.F. here now.'

'Q.R.F.?' the President asks.

'Quick Reaction Force,' Chandler responds as he draws his pistol, 'Come on, we have to leave right now, sir.' He walks up to the security door and swipes his card but nothing happens.

'Why isn't it working?' the President asks fear tinging his voice.

Chandler looks up at the ceiling, 'He cut the power.'

His eyes wide with fear, the President asks, 'How could this happen?'

Suddenly they hear a bang behind them. They both turn and look at the sealed door behind them. Then they hear another bang. 'What is that?' the President asks in a quaking voice.

'He's breaking through the blast doors,' Chandler responds grimly. Another bang rocks the hallway but it is closer this time. He aims his pistol at the door for a long eerie moment but nothing happens.

Suddenly Chandler drops to the ground, 'Get down sir,' he orders.

The President looks down at him in a moment of frozen panic but then the door suddenly comes hurtling off its hinges and crushes him. Chandler stares forward into the gloom but then he sees a pair of red eyes appear. He aims but the shadowy figure jumps straight upward through the ceiling. Suppressing a grimace, Chandler stands up and looks down at the President's limp leg sticking out from underneath the door. He presses a hand to his headset, 'Control, this is Chandler, we have a breach, I repeat, we have a breach. I'm proceeding to the rendezvous but first I need you to get the power on in here.'

A woman's voice comes on the line, 'Roger that commander, be advised QRF is en route.' Suddenly the lights flicker back on.

Chandler swipes his security card on the biometric scanner and hears the satisfying click of the door unlocking. He takes one last look behind him as the door opens but when he turns back he is suddenly confronted by the barrels of a whole squad of soldiers aiming at him. The platoon leader quickly stands up and walks over, 'Lower your weapons, he was with the President.' He turns to Chandler, 'What's the situation sir?'

Chandler turns to him, his eyes resolute, 'It's upstairs.'

Chandler stands in a rising elevator, surrounded by a fire team of heavily armed soldiers. His radio crackles and the voice of the platoon leader can be heard, 'Stairs clear', he reports but then they hear a muffled thud somewhere above them.

'He's moving, hold on stairs while we clear', Chandler says into his mic. The elevator comes to a halt on the second floor and the door slides open, revealing a darkened laboratory. The first two soldiers immediately cover the left and the right while the next two dash forward and clear the corners of the room. Chandler strides out into the center of the lab glancing around but there is no sign of their quarry. He raises his hand to touch his head set but then he notices dust and bits of plaster drifting down around him. He immediately looks up; weapon at the ready but only sees a hole in the ceiling from where Ravanna used his strength to punch through. 'He's on the roof!' Chandler yells as he sprints for the stairs.

He bursts out onto the facility roof, the wind whipping rain into his eyes as he clears left to right with his pistol but there's no sign of Ravanna, 'Where are you?', he murmurs as the other soldiers finally catch up to him and spread out. Suddenly the whine of a ship engine powering up can be heard over the din of the wind and rain. Chandler's eyes narrow as he runs over to the roof edge. He peers over the edge but then the President's shuttle suddenly lifts up into the air in front of him and roars overhead into the rainy night sky. Chandler watches in anger and humiliation before pressing his hand to his headset, 'He got out on the President's shuttle. Heading East but I think I can still get him.'

'Roger commander,' control responds over his headset. Behind Chandler three soldiers unpack a long sealed tube while two others set up a tripod. They attach the tube to the tripod and aim it at the fleeing shuttle, 'Ready to fire!' the soldier aiming the weapon announces.

'Fire!' his sergeant commands, but nothing happens. He looks over at the weapon operator in annoyance, 'What's wrong?'

'Something's interfering with the guidance laser,' the man responds.

The sergeant looks around for Chandler, 'Where the hell is the Commander?' he asks out loud. Suddenly he hears a deafening roar behind him but as he turns around he is blasted to the ground. Looking up in stunned admiration he sees Chandler fly overhead in a transport ship and then engage his afterburners and shoot off in pursuit of the Presidential shuttle's now dwindling tail lights.

Lightning flashes through the heavy cloud cover as Chandler accelerates the transport ship to its maximum speed. Looking ahead through the rain streaked cockpit canopy he can see the tail lights of the Presidential shuttle slowly getting closer but then he receives a burst of static in his earpiece, 'Commander, this is control, I'm receiving reports that the U.N. is going to DEFCON 1.'

Chandler frowns in annoyance, 'Why the hell are they doing that?

'They're not the ones who gave the order,' the voice in his ear says pensively.

Chandler's face grows pale as the sudden realization hits him in the gut, 'Ravanna,' he murmurs.

Suddenly his radio crackles again but then a gravelly voice can be heard on the other end, 'Pull back,' it mutters, barely audible over the roar of the engines and the pounding of the rain on the windshield. Frowning, Chandler asks hesitatingly, 'Who is this?'

Ignoring him, the tired, guttural voice repeats once again, 'Pull back.'

Chandler's stomach goes cold, his skin crawling as he peers out the windshield at the ship flying ahead of him, 'Is this ... Ravanna?'

'Yes,' the cold voice answers.

'Why are you doing this General?' Chandler asks in frustration.

'I had no choice,' the voice answers coldly.

Chandler frowns in confusion, 'I don't understand.'

'Perhaps one day I will explain,' Ravanna responds, 'However, if you do not pull back, I will be forced to use your own nuclear arsenal to destroy the entire planet.'

'And how do I know if I can trust you?' Chandler asks as he tries to control a growing sense of unease.

'You have no choice', the voice responds. Chandler frowns as he tries to think of a solution but then Ravanna breaks the silence, 'Pull back or else the earth is destroyed. Decide now.'

Chandler slams his fist down on the cockpit bulk head, 'Fine. I'm pulling back,' he growls angrily. The craft shudders violently as he quickly decelerates. He watches in frustration as Ravanna's ship rockets away into low orbit but then he receives another transmission.

The familiar metallic voice speaks once more into his ear, 'Soldier, tell me your name.'

Chandler frowns, 'That's not necessary General.'

The voice pauses as if in thought before responding, 'I remember your voice Aaron.'

'But we've never met,' Chandler says in confusion. How could he know who I am? Chandler wonders to himself but his sense of unease has suddenly turned into a cold dread rising from the pit of his stomach.

'I was there the day you were born,' Ravanna responds almost distantly.

Chandler looks at the microphone in even greater confusion and fear, 'How?'

'It's simple. I am your father,' Ravanna responds calmly.

Chandler looks incredulously at the ship ahead of him, 'My father committed suicide ten years ago.'

The metallic voice responds in a slow measured voice, 'When you were a small boy you couldn't sleep at night and kept waking up your brothers to play. Your mother got so frustrated with you that she tied you to your bed but after she went back to sleep I came and untied you and we spent the whole night playing together.'

'But you died,' Chandler says, his voice barely a whisper.

Ravanna pauses for a moment before replying, 'Not all deaths are permanent my son.'

Chandler suddenly feels a cold sweat begin to bead on his forehead, 'What are you going to do?' he asks fearfully.

'What I have to do,' the voice answers and above him Ravanna's shuttle activates its anti-matter engine and disappears into the vastness of space.

For a moment Chandler is almost overcome by the surrealism of it all but then his ear piece crackles to life, 'Commander, we have reports of missile launches all over the world.'

Looking down at the planet below he is shocked to see countless points of light suddenly blossom all along the horizon. Suddenly a silver point of light somewhere above him catches his eye. Looking up he sees a point of light flash on the surface of the moon before erupting into a huge supernova.

CHAPTER 2

A NEW WORLD

Valentine suddenly wakes up from a nightmare with a gasp and sits straight up. Looking around at the comfortable darkness of her bedroom the paralyzing fear of the night terror slowly dissipates. Next to her on the bed sleeps her reddish brown golden retriever Sam. He opens one eye and watches her as she takes a shuddering breath. Outside, she can hear the reassuring pitter patter of the rain on the window. And then finally with a sense of utter relief she plops back down into the warm comfort of her bed, 'Thank god it was just a dream,' she thinks out loud.

Standing in the shower with her eyes closed, Valentine lets the warm water wash away the stress of the dream world. Opening her eyes slowly she takes in the warm, earthy hues of the shower wall and wonders about the nature of her dream. 'Ollie?' she asks, 'Look up the meaning of a dream where you see the destruction of the world.'

The house based computer system whirs for a moment before replying in an aristocratic, English accented voice, 'To dream about mass destruction suggests that there is some chaos occurring in your life. Things may not be going the way you want it to. Perhaps the choices you are making are self-destructive.'

Valentine sighs to herself, 'Pretty spot on, I guess.'

'Is there anything else I may help you with Madame?' the computer asks.

'Yeah, get dinner ready,' she says as she rubs her face tiredly.

'And what shall I make?' the computer asks.

She smiles and turns off the tap, 'Comfort food.'

Valentine walks out into the living room neatly dressed. In the center of the room on a large circular table the Ollie computer hub system uses a multitude of black, stainless steel appendages to clean and dice vegetables. 'So much for the comfort food, Ollie,' she mutters as she passes by Sam. The dog looks up at her with his earnest yet gentle eyes and wags his tail in greeting as he lies down in his little bed and gets ready to go back to sleep.

'At Madame's age, I would think it wiser to minimize fatty acids and polyhydroxy aldehydes,' the computer answers enthusiastically.

Valentine shakes her head and rolls her eyes, 'I don't know what I would do without you Ollie.'

The computer whirs in thought, 'Madame would eat comfort food.'

Scanning the room, she spots a dark blue school bag thrown haphazardly across the couch, 'Ollie, is Jamie home?' she asks.

'Yes Madame,' the computer responds.

Valentine walks up a flight of stairs and gently knocks on a door, 'Jamie?' she calls but there is no answer. She opens the door, revealing a young boy's bedroom covered with posters, toys and clothes. Valentine pokes her head inside and looks around but the room is empty. Smiling to herself she walks over to the window and opens it. She sticks her head outside and finds her young son, Jamie, looking through a telescope at the twin moons rising into the evening sky, 'Hey Jamie,' she says happily as she carefully squeezes through the window and takes a seat on the roof.

'Hi mom,' he says as he glances at her but she can tell that there is something bothering him.

She frowns inwardly but decides to not press him just yet, 'Dinner will be ready soon.'

He doesn't seem to hear her and just keeps his eye on the telescope's eyepiece. Valentine turns to go but then stops and turns back to him, 'So are you trying to catch a glimpse of dad?' She asks enthusiastically.

Jamie turns and smiles, 'Yeah.'

Valentine kisses him gently on the top of his head as he presses his eye to the telescope eyepiece once again but as she turns to go back inside her eyes are glistening with tears. She takes a deep, shuddering breath and wonders how she will ever tell him that his father doesn't even know he exists and probably never will.

With his mom finally gone Jamie looks up from the eye piece of his telescope. The bright white light of the two moons begins to shine brighter as the dusk deepens but then he spots another little light twinkling. Something close to the planet's atmosphere by the look of it; he quickly places his eye against the telescope's eyepiece but is astonished to see a space ship slowly floating toward the planet. 'That is so cool,' he says excitedly as he takes a closer look.

Valentine drives her silver 2285 Series Mercedes Benz down a winding, paved forest road. The green blur of the wet forest whizzes by on either side of the car as some classical music from the local radio station blares from the car's speakers. Suddenly the song playing comes to an abrupt halt and the expressive voice of the station's DJ comes on, 'We interrupt this program to bring you a special bulletin from XFM Classical Radio,' the DJ pauses a moment as if collecting himself and then continues, 'Just a moment ago Government House announced that the Newport Observatory has reported an unidentified flying object approaching the planet's atmosphere. We are going to stand by for more info on this developing situation. Stay tuned to XFM Radio for further details.' The music starts up again but Valentine turns off the radio and frowns in consternation. Turning around another bend the car suddenly comes to a fork in the road, on her right Valentine can see the small, brightly lit town of Newport but she turns left and accelerates toward a large observatory on a hill in the distance.

Valentine speeds past an ivy covered sign that reads Newport Observatory before coming to the facility's security checkpoint. She rolls down her window and digs through her purse to get her ID but the guard walks up in a harried state of tension, 'Ma'am, they're all waiting for you. Better get inside quick.'

Valentine quickly walks down a brightly lit, beige hallway before coming to a door with a small blue screen next to it that reads Meeting Room A. She quickly tidies her hair and clothes before pressing her hand on the blue screen. It identifies her and the door silently slides open to reveal a full room of scientists, technicians and support personnel all sitting and standing in front of a huge screen displaying a star chart of their system. The head scientist stands at the front of the conference room, a laser pointer in one hand as he shows the trajectory the incoming craft took into the system, 'As you can see from this calculated trajectory we have reason to believe that the incoming craft is approaching from our old solar system, possibly a survivor of the destruction of the Earth.'

As the head scientist drones on Valentine edges her way through the seated scientists and sits down hastily. Suddenly one of the scientists stands up and, interrupting the head scientist's extensive monologue on the calculations used to measure the incoming U.F.O.'s trajectory, asks, 'So what proof do you have that this thing is actually from Earth?'

A group of voices murmur their assent and the head scientist turns to look at him, 'We have already re-tasked the telescope and taken some startling pictures.' He turns and nods to his assistant who changes the picture on the display. Suddenly Valentine's attention is drawn to the image that appears on the screen. A grey shuttle craft, mottled and flecked with age and decay, floats peacefully in orbit around their planet. 'As you can see,' the head scientist continues, 'the unidentified craft is of human origin. We have tried hailing the ship using a variety of methods but have received no response.' Suddenly the head scientist gets a call on his phone. He quickly answers and after listening intently for a few moments he hangs up and looks up at his audience in alarm, 'We have just received a new image of the U.F.O. It would seem we are now working under a time limit.'

'And why is that?' the scientist who had previously interrupted him asks incredulously.

The head scientist gives him a grim look, 'Change the slide,' he says to his assistant. The machine takes a few seconds to load the new picture but then it pops up on the screen. A woman in the crowd gasps. Standing in the cockpit viewport of the shuttle a tall, dark figure can be seen looking out at the camera. Valentine frowns as she studies the picture, a sense of dread slowly rising in the pit of her stomach. She is suddenly startled out of her reverie by the head scientist's voice, 'This is now officially a rescue mission. Are you ready to head up there Commander Valentine?'

Valentine sits strapped into the cockpit of the Nightingale S.T.S., one of the old fashioned rocket based space craft that the Newport Colony keeps on hand for emergency situations. Having already finished the A.P. computer startup configuration she has nothing to do but stare straight ahead through the cockpit's viewport into the overcast sky. Slowly, a frown creases her features as she finds herself wondering who the mystery traveler on the shuttle craft could be. She takes a deep breath and tries to still the deep seated anxiety stirring within her. The voice of the Launch Control Director comes on the radio, 'Nightingale STS, close and lock your visor and initiate O2 flow.'

'Copy' she responds shakily as she slides her helmet's visor down over her face and flips the rightmost switches on her pressure suit's control console. Almost immediately she can feel cool air begin to gently blow into the back of her flight

helmet. In her helmet ear piece she hears the ground crew fin-
ish their pre-launch status check.

'Guidance'

'Go'

'Hydraulic Pressure?'

'Go'

'Payload'

'Go'

'GPS'

'Go'

'Booster'

'We're Go'

'GNC'

'Go'

'CITO'

'Go'

'T –minus 17 seconds and counting, all systems are go,'
the launch director announces confidently.

Still nervous, she takes another deep breath and decides
to be logical about the situation, 'I'm the only qualified astro-
naut on this planet; it's up to me to either help someone up
there or to be the first line of defense for my world, for Jamie,
from whatever is out there.' She nods to herself, her face becoming resolute, 'We are go for auto sequence start', Valentine
says firmly in the mic.

In her mind she begins the countdown sequence, '10, 9,
8'. Underneath her she can feel the Nightingale's whole frame

begin to shake as the engines begin to power up, '7, 6, 5', then the engines actually power up and seem to drown out everything, '3, 2', suddenly the massive booster fuel tanks attached to the ship roar to life and the rocket lifts off at an incredible rate of 1900 miles an hour. A mixture of fear and excitement grip her as the shaking ship around her shoots through the clouds. After about a minute she can feel the computer's auto navigation alter the ship's course to a heading of 90 degrees and then prepares herself for the external tanks to separate from the primary module. A moment later the cockpit begins to shake violently as the tanks fall away to the planet below. Soon the shaking world around her disappears and she finds herself entering the peaceful black void of outer space. Slowly the force of the planet's spin slackens and then disappears altogether as the Zero-G effect takes over. Her legs and arms seem to rise into the air pulling at her restraints. Pulling off her flight helmet and stowing it she turns back to the viewport and speaks into her headset, 'Orbit good, beginning Hohmann transfer.'

'Roger Nightingale,' the flight director says nonchalantly.

Gunning the engine Valentine looks ahead through the viewport as her ship whips around the sphere of the planet. By using the gravitational pull of the planet's mass to slingshot her she races toward the dark side of the world below. As the rays of the sun falter and finally fade all falls to darkness in the cockpit around Valentine except for the yellow light from her instrument panels. Suddenly ahead of her and to the right she can see something dark, blotting out the stars, 'Control, I can see the target now, starting approach.'

'Roger that Nightingale, one more burn should do it,' control responds over her headset.

Using the lower orbit of her ship to increase her speed, Valentine hurtles forward at a speed of seventeen thousand miles an hour. Looking up she can see the black shape of her target passing by on her right hand side. With the darkened cockpit shuddering around her she studies the monitor that shows her position in correlation to that of the unknown ship. Nudging the control stick to the right she aims her ship at a point right in front of the other ship. 'Now,' she thinks to herself and guns the engine one last time to put herself in front of her target. The burst of energy launches her forward, pinning her to the seat. Suddenly she jams the brakes and gently pushes the control stick left. As the inertia of the sudden stop and turn spins the ship Valentine sees the planet below fly past through the viewport. She immediately tugs the stick right to counterbalance the spin and then suddenly finds herself face to face with the dark shape of the unknown ship perfectly in line for docking. Valentine stares at the other ship as a chilly sense of foreboding rises from within her. Forcing herself to think of how this will help to protect Jamie she speaks uneasily into her microphone, 'Control, I am now preparing to board the unidentified ship.'

The docking hatch seals with a thud and a stream of pressurized air. Valentine stands at the hatch, perspiration and fear beading on her frowning forehead. Wishing she had some sort of weapon just in case, Valentine takes a deep breath and presses her hand on the button that opens the hatch. The door slides open silently, revealing the darkened cabin of the other ship. A heavy stillness seems to hang in the dark humid air. She shines her flashlight inside but it appears empty, 'Hello?' she calls out hesitantly but there is no response. She takes her first steps into the other craft and immediately identifies the cockpit door. Fighting against the weightlessness of space she hops over to it and knocks, 'Hello?' she calls out once again, 'Anyone in there?' She listens carefully for any sound of response but the entire ship seems to be permeated by an eerie silence. Pressing her hand on the door it opens to reveal the cockpit but it is devoid of any life. 'Where is the man from the image?' she wonders to herself, 'Was it just some trick of the light?' Shining her flashlight around the room she finds the ship's computer and turns it on. It whirs to life after a moment and then the screen flickers on. Valentine studies the startup screen for a moment before asking aloud, 'Computer, what is the ship's point of origin?' The computer processes her request and then displays a 2-d image of a star map. A shining blip appears on the map showing the ship's current location by her home planet in the Wolf 359 system. As she watches in rapt fascination a yellow line is traced backwards from the blip. It stretches backwards first to the colony at Sirius then further back to the original colony at Alpha Centauri and then finally to Earth. Valentine frowns in thought as the line stops there. 'In addition to the Earth, those are all the colonies we've lost communications with over the last 10 years', she realizes, her face becoming pale. Suddenly she hears something knock against a bulkhead somewhere behind her. She spins around in fright, shining her flashlight back into the docking cabin, but she doesn't see anything. She cautiously enters the cabin and looks around but it is just as empty as when she first entered. Then she hears it again, a dull thump against a bulkhead. 'It sounds like it's coming from the cargo hold,' she thinks to herself as she frowns in dismay. She grips her flashlight tighter in her hand, forces herself to think of Jamie and then slowly trudges down the hallway that leads to the rear compartment. As she walks slowly toward the door she begins to hear something emanating from the hold. At first she can't quite make it out but the closer she gets the clearer the sound becomes. 'Is that what I think it is?' she wonders. She presses her ear to the cold, wet wall and listens as the indistinct sound becomes a slow throbbing thump, thump sound. 'It sounds like a heartbeat,' she realizes suddenly. Dread slowly rises in the pit of her belly as she finally reaches the door. Her heart is now pounding and with a shaking hand she uses the last of her willpower to reach out and open the door. Water immediately seeps out of the now open door onto her feet; she shines her flashlight in and sees a cryo sleep capsule with a shadowy figure inside. She slowly walks closer to get a better view. Water drips from the side of the capsule as she finally reaches the cloudy glass and tries to get a better view of the person inside. Raising her flashlight, she peers closely through the glass until her nose is almost touching the cold exterior. She frowns as the dark shape inside suddenly moves. Is that the man from the image she wonders to herself but then it moves again and bumps against the glass. Valentine screams in horror as a ghastly white face presses up against the other side of the glass and looks directly at her through dead unseeing eyes.

CHAPTER 3

THE SPACE SHERIFF

Neon lights shine through the rain as a man cloaked head to foot in a black rain coat walks toward a rundown night club. Music, laughter and gun shots ring out in the night air as he reaches the entrance and peers around carefully. He pulls the door open but the sound inside is almost deafening as he walks through a black lit hallway and out into an empty dance floor. Looking to the left he sees a darkened bar crowded with people. Suddenly one of the men lifts a small pistol in the air and shoots into the ceiling as a woman screams in fright and harsh, raucous laughter breaks out. Without uncovering his head, the man saunters over and finds a place at the bar. The bar keeper walks over and gives him a guarded but inquisitive look. Yelling to be heard over the deafening bass the man says, 'Medium Black Jack.'

The bar keeper nods in response as the man turns around and leans on the side of the bar. He looks out from under the hood of his rain coat at the group of loud men drinking to his left. One of them suddenly brandishes a silver pistol and shoots the drink out of the hand of a man talking to a woman nearby. The woman screams as the man falls to the ground in fright. The shooter and his friends laugh rowdily as the final remaining patrons quickly leave the bar. Then out of the black lit hallway a particularly large man emerges and seeing his belligerent friends walks over. He passes by the man in the rain coat but then he suddenly falls to the ground in a heap. Jumping up quickly he immediately turns his beady eyed gaze on the cloaked man and pulls out a large black handgun. Suddenly in a flash of movement the man throws his cloak off and reveals a green Sheriff's uniform and a huge sawed off shotgun trained at the man's chest. A name tag on his left breast pocket reads, 'Robert Renault'. The large man looks up at him in shock as the loud bass track is suddenly punctuated by the blast of the shotgun. The group of drunken men suddenly pull out their pistols but the Sheriff guns down the entire group with one massive blast. The shell also takes out the sound system and the deafening bass finally turns off. The Sheriff looks around for any more threats but then he hears a click behind him. He spins around and brings the shotgun to bear but he finds the bar keeper aiming a pistol at him, his hands shaking.

'Drop it!' he yells as he chambers another shell.

The bar keep hesitates for a moment but then he glances into the cold, pitiless eyes of the sheriff aiming at him and he quickly places the pistol on the bar and steps back. The bar keeper stands shaking with fear as he stares at the Sheriff but then he relaxes and lowers his shotgun. He pulls out his wallet and pays for his drink, 'You should think about getting out of town,' the Sheriff says gruffly as he walks back out the way he came. Glancing around at the bodies and smoking holes in the walls the bar keeper pours himself a drink with shaking hands.

Sheriff Robert Renault breathes in the cool night air as he walks up to the brightly lit entrance of the New Star Casino but then the door man stands up as he approaches, 'You're late Sheriff,' he says, a mocking tone in his voice, 'the boss ain't gonna like that.'

Robert merely nods as he walks past and enters the warmly lit interior of the casino. He walks through the practically empty establishment making a beeline straight for the heavy security door on the far side of the room. A small camera above the door aims down at him before he finally hears the click of the door unlocking. The door swings open and Robert walks down a long dank hallway before coming to another security door. Pressing a hand on a rather antiquated biometrics scanner he waits for it to read his fingerprints. Finally, the machine clears him and the door opens to reveal a massive drug lab. As he steps inside he is greeted by the loud din of processing centrifuges and a guard holding a bullpup style assault rifle. Robert nods to him and then walks up to a corpulent man standing nearby. The short fat man glares at a chemist in a white lab coat, 'Either get it up to twenty-five percent or I'll find someone who can,' he growls as he turns to Robert but then his eyes narrow in anger, 'You were supposed to take out two birds with one stone. Why didn't you kill the club owner?'

Robert looks down at him coldly, 'That's not what I do.'

'It's exactly what you do,' the Boss says as he glares back up at him, 'he was the owner of an establishment that is currently taking business away from me. That makes him my competition and therefore your problem. Unless of course you and I now have a problem?' the small man asks sardonically, 'Or are we no longer partners?'

Robert looks down at him, 'No,' he says, calming down, 'we're still partners. Just save the assassinations for your thugs.'

The Boss gives him a piercing look before finally grinning, 'Fine, but you're going to have to handle the security at the next deal we're having,' he says as his eyes harden once again.

'Where is it? Robert asks coldly.

'It's on some mining colony, the Wolf sector, I'll have the coordinates beamed up to you,' the small man says absent mindedly as he pulls out a package and hands it to the sheriff.

Robert opens it carefully but it is loaded with small but brilliant black diamonds. He gives the Boss a cold smirk,

'Now that is something I can do,' he says with a twinkle in his eye, 'I have absolutely no problem killing criminals,' he says as he walks out of the casino but the Boss doesn't smile as he watches him leave.

In the infinity that is space, suns are but grains of sand. A white dwarf star is barely worthy of notice and a small spacecraft like the FAC Athens is almost too tiny to exist in such emptiness. As it drifts through the great nothing Robert sits back in the cockpit of the Athens and stretches his legs out, sighing with satisfaction as he looks out the cockpit into deep space. He clenches a cigar in his teeth as he pulls a plasma-lighter from his pocket and lights the end. Pulling on it until it starts to burn, he exhales and watches the smoke rise to the ceiling but as he looks out into the vastness of space his eyes suddenly tighten with pain as the smallness of his existence hits him. He suddenly finds himself remembering a time when he had been young and married. And he realizes that he longs for it above all else. Taking another long drag on the cigar he exhales before slowly standing up and stretching. He puts out the cigar and places it in an airtight container. Suddenly the ship computer rings out an alarm. The computer whirs for a moment as it decrypts the light speed message but when the message displays on the screen it suddenly gives him goosebumps; the coordinates: 'X: -1.90, Y: -3.90, Z: 6.46', are for Wolf 359, his home planet.

Robert stands in the patrol ship's armory and quickly straps on his dark green Sheriff's department body armor. Inspired by the scales of a fish, the armor is made up of trillions of Nano sized gel filled scales that cover his torso in a light, flexible material that can stop anything from an old fashioned bullet to the more modern rail gun projectiles that can travel up to 12 miles in one second. Making sure that his armor is securely fastened he now turns to the armory gun rack but there is only one weapon available. Only about a foot and a half long, Robert bends down and deftly picks up the Alpha Centauri Systems SA 20 Para Light Machine Gun. Considered the most sophisticated hand held weapon in human history the SA 20 can fire a stunning 2000 mini ball rounds a minute using the electrically powered rail technology. Next Robert lifts the heavy but powerful interstellar radio transmitter and puts it on like a back pack. Placing a head set over his head he looks up, grim determination on his face, as the ship's computer alerts him that they have finally arrived at their destination.

The Athens slowly moves into position above the stormy atmosphere of Wolf 359. Robert stands at the observation port looking down at the turbulent weather systems below, 'Computer, land the ship,' he orders. The computer chimes in reply and then he feels as the ship begins to slowly move toward the planet. As it passes through the atmosphere the super structure around him suddenly begins to shudder from strong gusts of wind and the view port is sprayed with rain. Robert watches in rapt fascination as the ship silently approaches a wall of cloud and mist. Although the planet had long ago completed its atmosphere construction process it was still almost constantly blanketed by cloud formations and rain. As a boy Robert had loved to lie in bed at night with a flashlight and a book, exploring new worlds as he listened to the sound of the rain tapping against his window. Ahead through the mist Robert suddenly sees the forest of imported earth trees and in the distance at the edge of the horizon lays the planet's great obsidian mountains. As the ship circles around overhead Robert peers down intently through the viewport and spots three ships landed in a clearing in the forest. The computer analyzes the terrain and searches for a suitable landing spot while Robert turns and walks briskly down a hallway to the airlock. He feels the ship maneuvering into position and he begins to calm down and focus. Suddenly the ship lands with a jolt, the airlock depressurizes and the hatch falls to the muddy ground with a sickening thump. Robert is immediately greeted by a rush of cold, refreshing air. He cautiously peers out of the hatchway and looks around. The Athens sits in the middle of the large clearing surrounded by towering pine trees that sway in the cold wind. Glancing around furtively he looks at the three other ships but the landing field is completely empty. Stepping out onto the grass covered clearing he looks from left to right for any sign of anyone but the landing site is deserted. Walking through the cool evening air he inspects each of the three space ships in turn but they are all empty.

He steps off the last ship's landing platform and back onto the cold wet ground when he hears an odd call come from somewhere in the surrounding forest. Turning his head sharply he suddenly hears an answer come from the other side of the clearing. Looking around at the dark forest he doesn't see anything or anyone but then the dull boom of a ship entering the atmosphere reverberates through the air. 'Who could that be?' Robert wonders to himself as a small dilapidated transport ship flies overhead. The ship circles once before landing nearby. Robert makes his way over to the ship cautiously as the ramp drops and a very tall man falls to the ground. He laughs as he scrambles back up to his feet but as Robert approaches he can smell the stench of alcohol. 'Oh crap its Friday isn't it?' the stranger asks in a heavy Australian accent as he pulls a bottle of whiskey from his pocket and takes a swig. Wiping his mouth, he looks up at Robert, 'would you explain to my boss that Fridays are for drinking?' Robert doesn't answer as he raises an eyebrow. 'Never mind,' the man says, his words slightly slurred, 'I'm here now that's what matters, yeah?' He looks around, his eyes slightly unfocused. 'Hey mate, I got a question for you.' Robert crosses his arms impatiently as he looks down at the drunk but then the man's face becomes livid, 'Where the hell is everyone?' he asks with a snarl.

Robert smiles good naturedly as the man attempts not to throw up, 'That's a good question.'

The man frowns, 'What? Where they...' but his sentence is suddenly interrupted as he throws up on the ground.

Robert pulls out a small case full of different colored capsules and hands a bright red one to the man, 'Here buddy take this.'

'Ah my man, you're a life saver,' he slurs as he pops the capsule into his mouth. The man's face turns very pale for a moment and then very red but then he smiles and stands up.

'Just take it easy,' Robert says calmly as he glances around at the surrounding forest again, 'something's not quite right here.' Suddenly the man stands up, his eyes alert, his hand ready on a small carbine slung from his shoulder. 'Interesting,' Robert thinks to himself as he looks the odd man up and down, 'I guess he's not as useless as he makes himself out to be.'

'I didn't see any lights on in the town as I was coming in,' the man says in a low voice.

'What do you think is going on?' Robert asks curiously as he glances at the tall stranger once again. 'He looks like he's been in the military,' Robert judges silently.

'Same thing that's been going on in a lot of other colony worlds,' the man says once again in his low calm voice.

'What's that?' Robert asks concernedly.

'Doesn't matter now,' the man says, 'I know these signs. A little too well for my liking and I think it's high time we leave mate.' Suddenly they hear the strange call Robert heard earlier. Robert scans the forest as he looks for any movement but then the man grabs his arm. 'They're here,' the man says his eyes wide with fear as he turns tail and sprints into the gloom of the forest.

'Wait!' Robert calls after him but the strange man is gone. 'Who's here?' he wonders worriedly. He stands still for a moment, listening, but then he suddenly gets shot in the back. The force of the round knocks him down but Robert can feel that it didn't penetrate his armor. Ignoring the pain, he rolls onto his back and sprays a huge burst of fire in the direction that the shot came from but then a hailstorm of rounds land all around him in a flurry of impacts. His heart now suddenly pounding, Robert jumps up and immediately dashes into the cover of the nearby forest. The firing stops but as Robert sprints through the dense underbrush of the forest he suddenly hears the calls and war whoops of dozens of men chasing after him. He glances behind him and sees shadows crashing through the underbrush. Gulping in sudden fear he feels his adrenaline surge through his body as he runs as fast as he can. Dodging through low hanging branches and tripping through bushes Robert hears his pursuers getting closer and closer. He breaks through a dense stand of bushes but then he sees the white light of the moons lighting up a clearing ahead and beyond that the town of Newport. Suddenly a hand grabs at him from behind the bushes. Robert scampers out of reach of the clawing hand and runs for the clearing. The skin on the back of his neck crawls with fear as he crashes through the forest. Dark shapes seem to close in all around him as Robert accelerates the final few yards and finally bursts out into the clearing. The twin moons shine out overhead as he runs through the grassy field but when he glances back there is no sign of his pursuers.

A light drizzle falls swaying this way and that with the wind as Robert runs tiredly through the empty streets of downtown Newport. On the other side of the town lay the colony's landing field and Robert's only hope of escape from whatever was happening on Wolf 359. 'Whatever it is,' he thinks anxiously as he peers into looted and abandoned buildings, 'it isn't something I want to stick around and experience firsthand. I'd rather read about it in the news. If I can just get off this rock quickly and quietly nobody'll be the wiser.' He turns onto the main thoroughfare and arrives at the tall, imposing city hall building just as night begins to settle on the town. But then he remembers his sheriff patrol craft parked next to the three drug loaded ships in the forest. He stops dead in his tracks as he looks up at the ornate columned entrance of the building. Often during his tenure as the system sheriff Robert had had to ride that thin line separating criminal from cop. Working with the criminals had been his only way of staying alive on the corrupt colony worlds but sometimes you also had to work on the other side of that fuzzy line in order to keep yourself from falling completely down into the deep dark abyss of the criminal world. 'By waiting for the rest of the Wolf 359 taskforce I can just say that I was checking out those ships before I got chased here,' he plans silently to himself. Looking back up at the city hall entrance he thinks,

'Might as well see if I can find any clues about what's going on here.' Glancing around nervously, he takes a deep breath and then enters the darkened entrance.

Robert methodically clears through the darkened, abandoned halls and offices. He comes to a door marked Detective Thomas McKenna. Slowly opening the door, he peers inside but the room is almost completely empty except for a desk with an old fashioned desk top computer on it. He enters and says, 'Computer, display recent case files'. He stands in silence for a moment but then he remembers that you have to do everything manually with these older models. He bends down and quickly finding the power button turns it on. Robert opens the case file manager and looks up the most recent case. He frowns as the computer shows that the latest case on file is marked 'Disappearances'. He hurriedly opens the file but it is a video recording.

An aging, weather worn man appears on the screen smoking a cigarette, 'Went out to the Observatory yesterday, I'm almost sure they're lying to me,' the detective takes a long drag from his cigarette, 'I'm just not sure what they're hiding. I think the recent disappearances are somehow connected with that derelict space ship that was brought in. First, that strange ship appeared, and then out of nowhere people start disappearing. I know they're up to something at the institute I just can't be sure what it is.' The video ends and Robert, ready to finally find out what happened, clicks on the next file. Once again the grim looking Detective McKenna appears on the screen, he hurriedly puts out a cigarette and begins his report, 'The frequency of the crimes has increased and the chief had to call it in. But I did find my first clue. After a thorough re-examination of the first crime scene I have discovered trace amounts of an aerosol based chemical which I believe was used to quickly subdue the victim. I have sent it to the lab but I'm still waiting to hear back. Hopefully we can …'

Robert listens intently but the recording has stopped. He looks at the screen but a message has popped up, 'The file or directory is corrupt and non-readable. Please Run the Chkdsk utility.'

Robert scowls in annoyance as he turns to leave but then something on the wall next to the door catches his eye. Pointing his flashlight toward it he sees that it is a chart of all of the suspects in the recent disappearances. He walks over to get a better look but is suddenly shocked when he sees that the prime suspect at the top of the list is none other than his ex-wife Valentine.

CHAPTER 4

THE VISITOR

Robert runs along the road to the town landing field, holding his hand to his headset he attempts to use the interstellar radio strapped to his back to try and get help, 'This is Sheriff Robert Renault with Taskforce Wolf 359, requesting immediate assistance at coordinates X: -1.90, Y: -3.90, Z: 6.46'.' He waits for a moment but only receives static. He glances up at the overcast sky, 'Weather is messing with the signal. I need to get to a ship and use the communications array to get help.' As he hurriedly trots along under the rising moons he can't help but wonder why Valentine is not only considered a suspect but the leading one at that.

Almost out of breath now he finally reaches the landing field and to his relief finds several ships parked on the wide grassy expanse. He bends over, trying to catch his breath but when he looks up he sees it. Walking around the closest ship to get a better view his nervousness begins to cascade into genuine fear. Every single ship's communications array has been completely mangled beyond use. Robert stands stunned as he tries to think of a solution.

'So you noticed it too eh?' a voice with a strangely familiar Australian accent says from behind him. Robert turns and finds his drunken acquaintance from before giving him a grin. 'Good to see the boogey men didn't get ya.'

'Are the rest of the ships like this?' Robert asks as he glances around at the other ships.

'Might as well get comfortable,' the man says as he pulls out his bottle and takes a swig, 'we're not getting off this rock mate.' He offers the bottle to Robert but he shakes his head.

'I need to keep a clear head,' Robert says as he looks around for some inspiration or idea for how they can escape.

'Don't know why you'd want to do that,' the stranger says with a laugh, 'so you're the Sheriff eh?'

Robert nods, 'Call me Robert.'

'Yeah roger that Robert,' he says with a snort, 'you can call me Tommy.'

Robert turns to him and gives him a piercing glare, 'So I've been meaning to ask you how you knew we were about to get attacked earlier.'

Tommy gives him a little laugh, 'I'm a very well read individual you see,' he says mockingly.

, 'Oh I understand,' he says sardonically as he places a hand on his gun, 'I also like to stay well informed.'

The big Australian smiles broadly at him, 'Just 'cause you wear the uniform sheriff doesn't mean I have to tell you nothin. Last I checked real police men don't enforce drug deals yeah?'

Robert's eyes grow icy as they stare each other down but then he is startled by the clap of a sonic boom and then another, 'That's a ship,' he says as he looks up into the night sky. Suddenly a patrol ship screams by overhead. The small, one-man ship quickly circles the town but then it seems to spot him and lands nearby. 'That's military grade,' Robert says as he examines the ship.

'Yeah, except that model isn't supposed to be for interplanetary travel. It's a custom job,' Tommy says quietly.

Robert glances over at him, 'Who is this guy?' he wonders to himself.

Tommy catches him looking and gives him a wink before as he walks a few meters to the left and kneels down, 'I'll let you take care of this one sheriff.' A man in a military field kit steps out of the ship and waves at him. Robert runs over to him calling out, 'I'm the sector sheriff. We have a code 30 emergency going on here,' but he stops as the man threateningly raises his weapon.

'Hold up there,' the man says in a calm voice but for a moment Robert detects a look of intense fear in his eyes, 'I'm going to need to see some ID before we go any further.'

Robert studies him for a moment longer but the other man has seemingly regained his composure. Robert reaches into his cargo pocket on his thigh. 'Slowly now,' the man says tensely.

Robert grabs the ID and pulls it out, 'Are you with the Wolf 359 taskforce?' he asks.

The man smiles slightly, 'Just go ahead and place it on the ground and then take 10 steps back.'

Robert obeys him and then watches as the stranger cautiously walks forward and picks up the ID. He inspects the picture and then compares it to Robert, 'Looks real enough,' the man concludes, 'I'm Dr. Tillman with sector intelligence, here as part of the system wide search effort for the outlaw Dev Rickard. Who's your friend over there?' He asks as he glances over Robert's shoulder at Tommy who has now resumed his drinking.

Placing his ID back in his pocket Robert adds, 'He's a civilian I bumped into. It seems like everyone else is either dead or gone.'

Tillman looks at him in surprise, 'What? Why?'

Robert says, 'Something's happened here, I got attacked when I landed and the town's been abandoned.'

'Damn,' Tillman murmurs under his breath, 'I should have gotten here sooner.'

Robert looks at him suspiciously but he doesn't press him, 'I've been trying to call for help but all comms have been sabotaged.'

Tillman quickly turns and scans the area for any threats before turning back to Robert, his face now grim, 'Come on, let's use my radio.' Robert turns to call for Tommy but Tillman gives him a warning look, 'It will just take a minute. He'll be fine out here.'

Tillman leads Robert inside but then he quickly presses a button and the hatch closes behind him. Sensing a trap Robert lifts his gun but Tillman already has a pistol to his head. He says, 'Slowly now. Set your weapon on the deck.' Robert slowly sets his gun on the deck of the ship and then stands up and looks at his captor but his eyes have grown icy cold. Tillman tosses Robert a pair of hand cuffs. Pointing above him Tillman says, 'Secure yourself to that pipe.' Robert does as he is instructed but his nervousness has now been replaced with a slowly growing anger. Tillman leans forward to check them but then Robert swings his arms downward and knocks him to the floor. Tillman hits the deck hard and his gun flies out of his hand and slides across the metal floor of the ship. Tillman tries to shake off the concussion of the blow but then he sees Robert diving across the hold to grab the gun. Robert grabs the pistol and turns around to aim at Tillman but then he gets slugged across the face. Once again the pistol flies through the air before banging against the ship bulkhead and falling to the ground heavily. Tillman makes a dive for the gun but falls short as Robert grabs his legs from behind. Tillman kicks him heavily across the face and Robert releases him with a grunt of pain. He turns to the ship command console behind him and then he suddenly gets an idea. Tillman desperately dives forward and picks up the weapon but when he turns around he suddenly finds Robert aiming one of his own pistols at him. 'I thought you might have a backup hidden somewhere around here,' Robert says with a pained smirk.

Tillman cringes as he waits for Robert to shoot but nothing happens. Looking up at Robert curiously, he asks, 'Well what are you waiting for?'

'I want answers,' Robert demands icily.

Tillman snorts, 'What do you want to know?'

'For starters why don't you tell me your real name,' Robert says.

With a twinkle in his eye his prisoner stands up and calmly says, 'My name is Chandler.'

Suddenly the ramp drops behind them but as they both turn in surprise Tommy stumbles up into the ship and exclaims slightly tipsily, 'What the bloody hell is going on in here?'

Robert, Chandler and Tommy stand around the bridge computer. Chandler looks at him apologetically, 'I'm sorry about before but I needed to know what side you were on.'

Robert gives him a sardonic look, 'I'm still not even sure what side you're on.'

'Well I'm sure as hell not on either of you bloody bastard's sides,' Tommy says as he sits down in the corner and watches them both suspiciously.

Chandler smiles slightly and then turns to the communications console, 'Now then, let's see if we can make contact.' He presses a button on the console and brings up the radio frequencies for several nearby bases. Robert watches intently as he selects Barnard Star Command.

Suddenly a voice comes over the radio, 'This is 504 PIR, if anyone on Wolf 359 can read me respond, over.'

Chandler says, 'This is Wolf 359. Do you read me?

'We hear you loud and clear Wolf. What's the situation down there?' The voice responds.

'Situation is critical,' Chandler says, 'we need all available assets redirected here, over.' He waits for a response but all they can hear is static.

Robert looks at him, 'What just happened?'

Tommy mutters, 'He must've jammed the transmission.'

'So can you at least tell me who exactly is doing all of this?' Robert asks in confusion as he looks from Tommy to Chandler.

Chandler doesn't appear to hear him and just looks down in deep concentration, 'Why would he allow us to call for help if he has the power to jam us? For some reason he wants a paratrooper regiment to come here but he doesn't want them to know what they are walking into.'

'Can you jackasses quit playing the pronoun game?' Robert asks as his impatience starts to get the better of him.

Chandler nods to himself as if finally coming to a decision. He holds up a hand sized computer screen with a map of the colony and the landing zone, 'We'll use this.' He follows a little blip on the screen, 'It says the source of the jamming is coming from this location about 200 meters to the north west of the observatory. That's where we'll find him.'

'Seriously?' Robert says with a look of deep annoyance,

Chandler takes a long deep breath before looking up at Robert, 'His name is Ravanna,' Chandler finally states boldly, 'and he destroyed the Earth.'

CHAPTER 5

THE FOREST

Robert walks some distance ahead of Chandler and Tommy through one of the many dense stands of trees that make up most of the terrain around Newport. About 500 meters away Ravanna, the alleged world destroyer, was jamming the radio frequencies and that was all there was to the pre mission brief. With a sigh of resignation Robert bends down and looks up as the wind peacefully blows through the trees overhead. Taking a deep breath of the cold but refreshing air he slowly stands up and turns to find Chandler and Tommy giving him a curious look.

'What is it?' Chandler asks.

Robert looks at him but he can't hide his concern, 'I'm not sure we're going about this the right way.'

Tommy gives Robert a keen look, 'Well you're the native here sheriff, what do you think is the best way to approach the jamming source?'

'I think,' answers Robert slowly, 'I think the best thing is to go as straight westward from here as we can,' he says as he points to a line of foot hills in the distance, 'instead of directly for the target. From there we can use a path I know that runs behind them; it will bring us to the source of the jamming from the north and we'll have some more cover going in.'

'Makes sense to me,' Tommy agrees as he hefts his carbine up on his shoulder and continues plodding along. Chandler nods slowly as if thinking to himself before looking up at Robert and smiling slightly in approval but Robert can't help but notice a certain wariness in his eyes.

And so they plod along narrow forest paths, the twin moons slowly rising up into the deep blue of the late evening sky. The forest around them is largely silent except for the piping and wailing of a few melancholy birds. They finally reach the spur of foot hills extending from the roots of the massive obsidian mountains in the distance. The hills made an undulating ridge, often rising almost to a thousand feet, and here and there falling again to a low cleft or pass leading into the western forest beyond. Crossing through one of these passes they suddenly find themselves on the other side and then find for the first time since they had left the landing field, a track plain to see. Making a ninety degree turn they step onto the path and follow it northwards. The path, as it was known to the inhabitants of Newport, was an old one. Connecting the town to the all-important mines in the distant mountains the path was as old as the colony itself. Robert was very familiar with it, having once used it to explore the forest and the foothills as a youth. He turns to check up on Chandler but to his surprise the older man is completely out of breath.

'Are you okay?' he asks.

'Yeah, let's take a little break,' Chandler says as he drops to the ground.

'Sounds good to me, I'm starting to lose my buzz,' Tommy answers as he leans against a tree and takes a sip from his bottle.

'So who exactly is this Ravanna?' Robert asks, his curiosity finally getting the better of him, 'I know that both you guys are holding out on me.'

Tommy looks at him for a moment before taking a big gulp from his bottle and then cringing. Chandler sighs, 'All we know is that he's a rogue UN Special Forces general. When he took command during the cultist insurgencies of the twenties they had been going after the families of all of the government troops sent against them. So in order to circumvent that, he made it standard operating procedure for all men and women under his command to have their personnel files erased and then issued a code name. It helped us win the war but it also helped him disappear after it ended.'

'And why did he disappear?' Robert asks.

'No one knows for sure,' Chandler says as he looks down, 'but there are some who have their own theories.'

Robert snorts sarcastically, 'And you wouldn't happen to be one of those people?'

Chandler stands up stiffly and looks at Robert, 'Trust me sheriff, you'll get all the answers you can stomach soon enough.' He turns and continues walking along the trail.

'Too right,' Tommy adds as he puts away his bottle and follows Chandler.

Robert stands stock still as he looks after them feeling a mixture of genuine curiosity and not a little apprehension of what's to come.

A light drizzle falls through the trees of the forest while to the East the twin moon's first white rays poke through the clouds overhead. They walk through the overgrown, wet forest but then Robert stops and crouches down. Ahead of them lies a clearing and further back begins the mountain's rugged foothills. He slowly scans the bushes and hills for any movement but all is still. He stands up cautiously but then a gloved hand quickly grabs his shoulder and forces him down. He turns in surprise but finds Chandler staring straight ahead transfixed. Behind him Tommy is turned around covering the rear with his carbine. Chandler slowly raises a finger to his mouth and then points ahead. Robert follows his line of sight, but then he sees it. His heart skips a beat as he looks at the dark figure squatted low beneath a tree 100 meters away on the crest of one of the foothills. Adrenaline suddenly flows through his body. He tries to make out the person's features but they are obscured by the shadows and foliage. A bird calls out somewhere in the forest as they stare ahead but then the shadowy figure crawls behind the tree and disappears. Behind Robert, Chandler softly whispers, 'The way is blocked ahead.'

Robert turns without looking at him, his forehead creased in worry, 'How do you know?' he whispers back hoarsely.

'Trust me,' Chandler whispers back knowingly.

Robert looks at him for a moment before turning back, 'What should we do?' he asks quietly.

'Where can we take cover around here?' Chandler asks thoughtfully.

His eyes still trained on the hill, Robert says, 'The Observatory is nearby.'

The three men walk through the now silent and dark forest. Overhead the twin moons and the stars shine through a lull in the usual clouds and rain. Their white light casts a luminosity that seems to tinge everything blue. Glancing up at the night sky Robert admires the view for a moment before turning his gaze back to the dark forest around them. He adjusts his pack and then continues up a particularly steep incline. Feeling his muscles burning from the exertion he finally reaches the top and finds the west side of the observatory only about twenty feet away. Scanning the building,

Robert looks for any light or sign of it being occupied but it appears to be abandoned.

Chandler and Tommy trudge up behind him. Robert glances back at him but Chandler silently raises a finger to his mouth and signals for them to move around to the entrance. Robert nods and carefully leads the way around the side of the building. They come to the glass doors of the front entrance but the interior of the building is completely dark. Robert looks to Chandler for guidance. He glances around the parking lot in front of the building before turning to Robert and gesturing for him to enter.

The three men silently walk through the darkness, straining their eyes and their ears for any sign or sound of danger. Suddenly Chandler and Tommy stop dead in their tracks. Robert stops too and looks around but then he hears it. Somewhere to their left in the darkness he can hear a soft whirring sound. They listen with all of their might. It sounds like the tiny gears of a machine moving. Chandler points a small flashlight at the sound and turns it on, the tactical red light of the device illuminating a small video camera. The lens on the camera whirs as it zooms in on them, 'I'd a feeling we'd find some more people in here,' Tommy murmurs as Chandler smiles and waves at the camera. Suddenly they hear a lock click on their right.

They turn and look but then a door opens, white light spills out into the corridor and to Robert's surprise a reddish brown golden retriever leaps up into his arms, 'Sam!' he exclaims as the dog licks his face happily, 'what the hell are you doing here buddy?' He turns to look inside the door as someone walks up but then he finds himself face to face with his old ex-wife Valentine.

'Crickey, I wasn't expecting a Sheila,' Tommy says in surprise, 'and a ranga at that,' he says with a laugh.

Valentine looks at him in confusion but Chandler steps in front of him, 'Don't mind him ma'am we're here to help.'

'Please come inside, it's safe,' She says with a look of gratitude before turning back to Robert. For a moment Robert and Valentine both stare in shock at one another as Chandler leads Tommy inside.

'Val,' Robert says in a soft voice as Sam drops to the ground and follows the others but then she suddenly grabs him in a fierce embrace. Robert stands in surprise but then a small boy of about eight or nine years walks up out of the door way and looks at him, beaming with excitement.

CHAPTER 6

A MEETING OF MINDS

Other than the soft white light of some security monitors the room is unlit as Robert, Chandler and Tommy stand in the warm darkness of the safe room. Valentine turns to Jamie, 'Hey Jamie why don't you go get these gentlemen some water bottles.'

'Ok mom,' he says excitedly as he runs down a hallway to the safe room's storage.

Chandler nods with a smile, 'Thank you ma'am. Are you sure there is enough to spare? We don't want to inconvenience you and your son.'

'Yeah, there's a year's supply in there,' Valentine says cordially.

Jamie stumbles out of the storage room with his arms full of huge water bottles but then they all tumble to the ground.

'Oh don't worry son,' Chandler says as turns, 'we'll take it from here.' He turns to Tommy, 'Come on let's help the kid.'

Tommy rolls his eyes, 'Fine, for the kid then,' he says as he puts away his bottle of alcohol. Suddenly Robert finds that Valentine has walked up and is standing next to him. A static energy seems to rise between them as he turns to her.

'Rob,' Valentine whispers as she looks up into his eyes and feels a mixture of conflicting emotions course through her. Wordlessly they search each other's eyes as they feel all the weight of their old relationship and the years that have gone by since they last saw each other. As the others walk up Valentine nods slowly and then turns to Jamie, 'Thanks for helping hun.'

'No problem mom,' he says as he looks up at Robert.

Robert looks down keenly at the boy for a moment before giving him a smile, 'I'm going to take a look around and make sure this place is secure.'

Robert turns on his flash light and walks down the hall while Chandler turns to Valentine, 'So how long have you two been in here?'

'It's been two days since things got bad and we had to come in here,' she says calmly as she watches Tommy sit down in the corner and pull out his bottle.

'Ace,' he says as he takes a sniff and then tilts the bottle forward. He tilts it forward even more but it's completely empty, 'ah hell, you've got to be kidding me,' he says in obvious disappointment. 'I was looking forward to that.'

Chandler grins at him, 'Looks like you're going to just have to keep on looking forward to it.' He glances around the room before turning back to Valentine, 'So how secure is this place?'

Valentine looks over at Robert before answering, 'It's probably as secure as you can get on this planet. Reinforced titanium walls and doors and down the hall there is an escape elevator that leads to the roof.'

Robert hears something behind in the darkness and turns to find Jamie looking up at him expectantly. He kneels down next to him, 'Hey man. How you holding up?'

'Okay,' the young boy says as Sam walks over and starts sniffing Robert's boots intently.

Robert sticks out a hand, 'You can call me Robert. What's your name?'

Jamie shakes his hand and gives him a wry smile, 'My name is Jamie,' he says quickly but then he looks at him impatiently, 'So can we leave now?'

Robert looks hesitant for a moment before answering, 'Well not yet. You guys can just stay here until it's time.' But Jamie looks extremely disappointed. Robert places a hand on his shoulder, 'Don't worry man, everything's going to be okay.'

'I know, I just thought it was over,' the young boy says despondently.

'Trust me,' Robert says, 'help is on the way.'

Jamie nods solemnly as Robert stands up and ruffles his long brown hair but then he notices Valentine looking at him wistfully. For a moment they look into each other's eyes but then the deep rumble of a double sonic boom shakes the room. Chandler looks to Robert, 'That's a cruiser,' he says before running out of the room.

'Finally, its high time we got off this rock,' Tommy says as he picks up his carbine and follows him out the door. Robert turns to Valentine as he follows but Valentine just gives him a concerned look. He runs out of the building and finds Chandler and Tommy standing in the middle of the observatory parking lot looking up into the night sky. Robert looks up too but then he sees a huge space cruiser flying towards them. Robert smiles and looks to Chandler and Tommy but their faces are grim. Robert frowns, wondering what could have them so concerned. But then he sees it, in the far distance a pair of lights streaking towards the ship. Suddenly it dawns on Robert, 'Ravanna's using the planet's anti-air defenses.'

'I should have known,' Chandler mutters angrily. The missiles strike the hull along the engines in a huge fireball. They watch in stunned silence as the ship starts to break apart but then they see dozens of escape pods jettison and fall to the surface of the planet as the ship crashes into the forest a couple hundred meters away in a huge explosion.

'God damn dead heads shouldn't have just flown straight in like that,' Tommy says as he shakes his head sorrowfully.

Robert turns to Chandler, 'We have to get out there.' But Chandler remains silent, a look of dread and apprehension on his face.

CHAPTER 7

DEVILS IN THE FOREST

One of the escape pods crashes down into the forest. Fire from the crash illuminates the forest night. The hull crackles with heat as the hatch opens and a paratrooper falls out. He tries to stand up but then he falls back down. He hears someone moving through the underbrush.

Coughing, he calls out, 'Is someone there? We need help!' The footsteps stop. He looks up and tries to peer through the smoke and rain but then several pairs of glowing green eyes appear.

Robert, Chandler and Tommy walk through the forest as the rain falls on them through the trees. Chandler stops and sinks to a knee. He turns to Robert and Tommy using hand signals to say that he can see an escape pod. Robert nods and they push up but there is no sign of the survivors.

Tommy looks around in confusion, 'Where are these drongos?' Suddenly they hear a twig snap behind them. They turn and aim as one but then they see a group of about 10 paratroopers aiming at them. 'There they are,' Tommy says with a smile as he puts down his weapon.

Chandler lifts his weapon into the air and calls out, 'Hold your fire! We're on the same side.' An older man with a small eagle on his uniform steps forward from the group, 'You the one we talked to on the radio?' he asks.

Chandler nods but then he notices a young machine gunner looking keenly at him. Looking back to the officer he says, 'Yeah, I'm Commander Chandler. I called it in.' The young man's eyes light up at the name but Chandler ignores him.

They shake hands as the other man says, 'Colonel James, 82nd Airborne.' Robert frowns as he remembers his old Captain James on Alpha Centauri. Could this be the same man who basically got him shot that fateful day when his life fell apart? He grimaces as he touches his old wound but no one else seems to notice.

Chandler looks around at the forest, 'Let's keep moving and try to gather as many survivors as we can.'

'Roger that,' the colonel says as he signals to his men. They set out into the rain but then they come to another escape pod. Robert pushes forward into the pod and shines his flashlight inside but it is completely empty. Walking outside he is slightly surprised to find the paratroopers are arrayed in a semi-circle around the escape pod.

'What's up?' he asks Tommy as he settles down next to him.

'What do you think?' the tall man says as he rubs his temples, 'god damn hangover, that's what's up.'

In the distance they can hear a sudden firefight erupt. Robert looks up as a group of paratroopers make their way over and take cover with them behind a large grass covered berm. The young man who had looked at Chandler so keenly crouches down next to him.

'Looks like we have company,' he says lazily as he glances up at Robert, 'I'm Reese'; he adds as he pulls out a cigarette and lights it with his plasma torch. He offers one to Robert but he shakes his head.

Reese pulls on the cigarette before asking, 'So you know the Commander? I mean Chandler?'

Robert says, 'Not really, I just met him.' Reese nods and sets up the bipod but he is shaking with fright. Robert suddenly feels an almost paternal affection for the young man, 'Don't worry kid. I won't let anything bad happen to you,' he thinks quietly to himself. They stare into the darkness and listen to the eerie warbling of a night bird and the steady drone of tree frogs. Suddenly a bullet whizzes out of the night, passing close by Robert's head. They immediately drop to the ground behind the grassy berm.

'Enemy front!' Tommy yells as he hits the dirt.

Robert lifts his head over the top to try and see who shot at them but then a series of distant pops can be heard in the distance followed by the whine and whistle of a fusillade of bullets passing right overhead, 'Whoa, whoa!' Robert exclaims as he ducks back down. He looks to Tommy but the Australian has a crazed look in his eye and laughs maniacally.

'Yes! This is what it's all about!' he says as he pokes his head up over the top and fires a few rounds from his carbine, 'Come on you bastards!'

'Cease fire!' Chandler yells down the line, 'that might be blue you drunk moron.' Robert looks to Chandler, his adrenaline pumping, but he is busy speaking calmly on a radio.

'Did you see him?' Reese asks Tommy excitedly.

'Nah, nah it's too dark,' Tommy responds with a grin, 'they're using low light contact lenses.'

'That's how they could see me,' Robert says, feeling nervous now. He looks down at his shaking left leg, 'Damn adrenaline always gives me the shakes,' he thinks in annoyance. As if to prove the point a pop in the distance is followed by another bullet zinging overhead. Robert looks to Chandler again in frustration, 'Hey can we open up?' he calls.

Chandler looks over at him, 'Negative, we have to make sure those aren't friendlies.'

'Roger,' Robert calls back, fear tinging his voice.

'They certainly ain't acting very friendly,' Tommy says with a laugh, 'hey mate let me get one of those cigs yeah?'

Reese pulls out the pack and throws it to him, 'Knock yourself out.'

'Cheers mate,' he says with a smile, 'if we can't shoot then I might as well have a smoke.'

Suddenly a series of pops and deep booms echo through the burning forest night as another volley of rounds zips by like a swarm of angry metal wasps.

'Ok those aren't friendlies,' Chandler calls out from down the line, 'open up.'

'Finally', Robert says in relief as Reese sets his heavy machine gun up on the top of the berm and begins to shoot bursts of explosive rounds that rock the very ground under their feet.

'There you go mate, let em have it,' Tommy says as he takes one final drag on his cigarette and throws it away, 'Oi Robbie whadda say you and I have a pop.' Robert nods and together they rise up from behind their cover and start placing rounds downrange into the darkness. Suddenly several rounds fly by. Robert and Reese immediately take cover but Tommy remains standing and returns fire calmly as enemy bullets and mini balls zip around him.

Robert and Reese look at each other incredulously and shake their heads, 'Is he crazy?' Reese yells over the din of combat.

'I'm certainly starting to think so,' Robert answers in a low voice as he watches the fearless Aussie shoot the last rounds in his clip and rejoin them. Having finally calmed himself Robert turns and looks down the line at Chandler who is nodding at one of the paratrooper NCO's. The NCO picks up a rocket launcher tube. All along the line all the men crouch down and watch in anticipation as the NCO walks to the top of the berm and aims. The rocket suddenly fires in an ear shattering blast and all of the men give a war whoop in response. The NCO calmly jumps down into cover as Robert pokes his head over the top of the berm. He looks up in awe at a massive mushroom cloud forming overhead but then a ripple catches his eye. The shockwave from the blast suddenly comes flying toward him and he barely manages to duck back down as it jolts the air overhead. He hears a laugh but when he looks he sees Tommy and Chandler smiling at him, 'Mate that was a two-thousand-pound warhead,' Tommy says with a grin. Robert sits down shakily and grumbles, 'Thanks for the warning,' Chandler doesn't say anything and Robert looks up at him but he is just staring forward into the dark forest. Robert frowns, 'You think he's using them to distract us?'

'I would bet on it. He's probably got elements flanking us,' Chandler agrees thoughtfully. He suddenly turns to the Colonel who has taken his place on the radio, 'Hey colonel if you give me a couple guys I'll cut off any flankers coming in.'

'Roger,' James says with a nod. He turns to the paratroopers and points to three soldiers, 'Get off your asses and follow the commander.' They obediently stand up and walk over.

Robert also stands up but Chandler gives him a look, 'Trust me, I got this one,' he says calmly as he places a hand reassuringly on Robert's shoulder.

Robert frowns, not fully understanding, 'You sure?'

Chandler nods with a forced smile, 'Yeah, you'll get the next one.' Robert watches with concern as Chandler turns and tramps into the forest with the three soldiers in tow.

The rain picks up as Chandler leads his three men through the forest but then they come to a field. Chandler turns to his guys and whispers, 'Hold here. Form a line.' The men form up and face the opposing tree line but all is quiet. A gentle breeze ripples through the tall grass of the field. Chandler turns to the paratroopers, 'I'm going to go do about two minutes of recon, be right back.' They nod as they slowly scan the field. Chandler quietly stands up and walks alone into the darkness of the forest behind them. Placing one foot gently in front of the other he silently makes his way through the wet undergrowth. He stops and crouches as he scans the darkness and listens intently. Then he hears it, a snap of a twig cracking underfoot. He begins blinking profusely as he stares into the dripping shadows of the forest. His skin crawls as he hears another crack, closer this time, and then the rustle of a body moving through the underbrush. Suddenly a pair of glowing green eyes appear and then another.

'I'm gonna go after Chandler,' Robert finally says out loud, 'I get the feeling he's going to try something crazy.'

'I wouldn't put it past him,' Tommy says thoughtfully, 'I've been around a lot of fighting men and I can tell the ones that have nothing to lose.'

'Speak for yourself,' Robert says with a grin as he quickly stands up.

He turns and walks off after Chandler but then Tommy calls after him, 'Oi Robby.'

Robert turns and gives him an inquiring look.

'Watch yourself mate,' he says with a look of genuine concern. Robert nods absentmindedly as he tramps off into the forest but Tommy turns to Reese, 'He has no idea what he's in for.' Reese looks up at him like he wants to say something but then he just shrugs and pulls out another cigarette.

Robert walks up on the three paratroopers manning an outpost but Chandler is nowhere to be seen, 'Where's Chandler?' he asks softly.

The corporal in charge whispers, 'The Commander is doing a little recon.'

Robert nods, 'I'll find him.'

He turns in the direction that the troopers had motioned toward and starts to follow a barely discernible track leading deeper into the forest. As he walks he suddenly becomes aware of how loud his footsteps plopping into the wet ground sound. Stopping, he looks around apprehensively. The forest around him has suddenly become deadly silent. The steady background drone of crickets and frogs had ceased abruptly for some reason. Searching the darkness for the cause he tries to listen for the sound of movement in the underbrush but he can only hear the faint whistle of the wind and the pitter patter of rain. Stepping off the path quickly and silently he gently lies down under the leaves of a large bush. As the branches of the big trees move in the wind, the moonlight from the twin moons filters through creating a dappled, shifting pattern. Then he hears it, the soft tread of bare feet. He freezes and slowly turning his head sees three dark shapes silently pass by within a foot of him. His heart pounding, Robert watches them disappear in the direction he just came from. Slowly the sounds of the forest return: the first tentative croak of a tree frog, the buzz of a cricket, and then the full chorus. Robert gets up quickly and starts running in the opposite direction. He makes it a safe distance and stops to catch his breath. He listens for any sounds of pursuit but he can't hear anything. He regains his composure and looks around but then he sees torches moving through the forest. Peering through the dense underbrush he suddenly feels his guts turn ice cold. In the flickering torch light, he can see Chandler being led by some men. He isn't restrained but Robert notices that one of his escorts is carrying his weapon. He squints as he tries to get a good look at Chandler's captors but they are covered in dark mud that resembles war paint. Robert quickly takes aim at the men with his SA 20 but they are too close to Chandler. He lowers his weapon in silent frustration as he watches them disappear into the night and then taking a deep breath he stands up and follows them into the darkness of the forest.

Robert slowly and carefully follows the torches until they come to a small cave entrance set at the base of one of the rising hills. As the torches disappear into the entrance Robert looks around apprehensively one last time before following after them into the black maw of the cave. He slowly walks into the darkness, careful to keep any sound to a minimum. He passes one side tunnel after another but the light from the torches continues down the main passage. The tunnel winds and turns as it continues farther and farther down. Suddenly he notices a dull rumble growing and then the bright white glow of electrical light coming from around a bend in the tunnel. He quickly steps to the edge of the bend and pokes his head around but he is amazed to find a huge subterranean excavation. He sees massive floodlights lighting the cavern as huge excavators dig out new chambers. Robert slips inside and conceals himself in the shadows of one of the excavators. He watches in breathless anticipation as Chandler is led to a raised command center set up in the middle of the chamber.

Chandler walks up a flight of stairs and out onto the top of the command center. A man in a black space suit stands with his back to him. He slowly reaches down and picks up a darkened space helmet and carefully places it onto his bald, scarred head. He turns around as the seals of the space suit lock into place and faces Chandler, 'My son, why have you come to me?'

Chandler looks at him in contempt for a moment but then his gaze softens 'I have come for the truth,' he says firmly.

'That is a noble cause,' Ravanna says as he strides forward, 'and what truth do you seek?'

'If you are my father, which I doubt, then I want to know how you're still alive,' Chandler says grimly, 'I saw your body.'

'Since that is part of the reason for why I destroyed the Earth then I will tell you.' Robert's ears perk up as he listens attentively from his hiding place. 'The human body does not actually die immediately after the heart stops. Long term memory, personality and identity are stored in durable cell structures and patterns within the brain that do not require continuous brain activity to die and persist for some time after what many considered legal death. You may have seen my body but you did not see them cryogenically freeze me for later use,' he spreads his hands, 'and this is the result.'

A pained look comes into Chandler's eyes as he stares at what remains of the father he once revered but Ravanna doesn't seem to notice, 'This was just one of the many travesties that I sought justice for against the United Nations of Earth. In the name of all they thought worth preserving those politicians and generals and admirals committed such atrocities that I had no choice but to seek revenge for all they had wronged,' he says bitterly, 'In order to create the perfect life on earth for their wealthy, indulgent citizens they created monsters.' Chandler stands silently as Ravanna, his face unreadable under his mask, walks up to him. For a moment he looks into the eyes of his son but he doesn't say anything. He turns to one of his men, 'Have you disarmed him?'

The man falls to his knees, 'Yes my lord.'

Ravanna turns back to Chandler but then he cocks his head to the side, 'And what about him?'

His minion looks at him in confusion, 'My lord?'

Ravanna points directly at Robert, 'Your friend that followed you in and is now hiding behind that excavator.'

Chandler spins around and looks at Robert in horror but then Ravanna raises a hand and sprays him in the face with a black gaseous substance that shoots out of a small hole in his palm. Chandler chokes a scream as he falls to the ground. Robert stands frozen in horror and surprise as he watches his friend spasm for a moment before lying still. Suddenly the screams and war whoops of the dozens of Ravanna's men sprinting towards him shakes him out of his stupor. One of the men, his body covered completely in dark mud, suddenly grabs him from behind. Robert puts all of his strength into elbowing him in the stomach and then shakes loose of his grip as he starts running to the tunnel. He barely makes it to the tunnel ahead of the mass of black painted men and starts sprinting through the darkness, his heart pounding as the tramping of many feet and the haunting yells of his pursuers echo in the confined space around him. Suddenly he sees the soft light of the moons and the end of the tunnel but then he feels something grab him from behind and he falls to the ground. Snapping his head back he sees one of Ravanna's men standing in a hidden trapdoor, the whites of his eyes shining in the darkness as he holds onto his legs. Robert kicks him across the face but then the man yells, 'Blow it!' and to his dismay the tunnel entrance collapses in front of him. Robert looks around in a panic as the sound of his pursuers draws ever closer. Turning to the right he spots one of the many side tunnels that he had passed earlier. Without a moment to lose he sprints down the passage, banging into the walls in his adrenaline fueled panic. A wooden door has been shoddily set up to block the way but he runs right through it without slowing down. Suddenly the tunnel slants upwards and to his relief he sees the glow of a fire emanating from down the tunnel. With his heart pounding and his body shaking he suddenly comes to a recently excavated cavern but to his horror it is filled to the brim with caged men, women and children. He pauses for a moment in shock as they all turn and look at him in terror but then Ravanna's men burst into the room. Without even another glance Robert sprints down another connecting tunnel and leaves them to their fate. This tunnel also continues up higher and higher. His legs are now burning with exertion but with the help of his adrenaline rush he pushes himself even faster and harder to escape. He sees another door ahead and crashes through it only to come to a sudden halt at the edge of a cliff overlooking the forest and in the distance the town of Newport. The sound of the pursuit nears once again and looking back one last time he flings himself off the cliff and into the darkness of the night.

CHAPTER 8

DEFENSIVE MEASURES

Robert suddenly wakes up in the warm darkness of the observatory safe room and sits straight up but then Valentine walks over and gently places a hand on his forehead, 'Don't worry. You're safe now.' Robert feels himself relax and sinks back down into the softness of the bed.

'What happened?' he asks as he looks into her clear blue eyes.

'Well you had a bit of a fall,' she says as she gives him a sympathetic look.

Robert chuckles softly to himself but it makes his chest hurt, 'I remember that part but everything after that is a little unclear.'

'The soldiers brought you back here about eight hours ago and then they left,' she explains as she sits down next to him, 'They said they were going to set up a base in the town.'

Robert nods to himself, 'Makes sense.'

Valentine turns around and grabs a bottle of water from a large storage container but then Robert suddenly recalls the list of suspects he saw in the detective's office, 'Val, I need you to explain something.'

'I'm afraid the soldiers didn't give me too much more info before they left,' she responds cheerily as she turns back around to face him.

Robert gives her a piercing glance, 'I stopped by the detective's office before we came here yesterday.'

Her face suddenly falls as she realizes that he knows, 'He takes control of you,' she says as her eyes well up with tears, 'I don't know how he does it. But he can make you do horrible things. It's almost as if you are watching yourself in a nightmare and there's nothing you can do.'

'How do I know you're not lying?' Robert asks sternly.

'Who do you think you were fighting out in the forest last night? They were your old neighbors and friends,' Valentine says as she looks at him earnestly.

Robert thinks back to the cages full of people that he saw in the cave and then he remembers the aerosol based chemical that Detective McKenna mentioned in his video.

Suddenly Jamie sticks his head inside the door, 'Sheriff Robert!' he exclaims as he runs up to the bed, 'Are you okay?' he asks.

Robert continues to stare at Valentine but his eyes have softened, 'Yeah kid. I'm feeling a lot better now.'

Jamie turns to his mother, 'Mom there are some soldiers at the door that want to come in.'

Valentine, suddenly feeling vulnerable, turns to her son as if noticing him for the first time and answers robotically, 'Thanks hun, I'll go let them in.'

She walks out into the control room and Jamie and Robert are left alone. Jamie gives Robert an inquisitive look, 'So did you fight the bad guys last night?'

Robert grins, 'Oh yeah, we…' he suddenly trails off as the haunting vision of Chandler falling to the ground unresponsive comes back to him suddenly.

Jamie doesn't seem to notice as he turns and looks as Valentine reenters with a paratrooper medic and Tommy in tow. Tommy grins lopsidedly at him, 'Heya mate! Good on ya for surviving that. I was sure I wouldn't see ya again.'

Robert smiles weakly, 'Thanks Tommy. You find anymore booze yet?'

'Nah mate, I reckon this has all been good for me,' he says happily, 'I'm as clean as a whistle.'

'Ah, that's too bad' Robert says as the medic pulls out a large syringe, 'I think I'm the one who needs a drink now.'

'Yeah, too right, now you know why I liked to get bombed out,' he says thoughtfully.

'You ready to get back in the action Sheriff?' the medic asks as he walks up and preps Robert's forearm.

Robert glances up at Valentine and gives her an understanding look, 'Yeah doc, get me back in the fight.' The medic quickly jabs the syringe into his forearm. Robert cringes in pain for a moment but then he suddenly feels a current of electricity run up and down his body. He spasms for a moment but then the feeling passes and Robert feels his body come to life like never before. Sitting up he places a hand on his chest but the swelling and pain are already diminishing.

'Come on,' Tommy says to the medic, 'let the bloke get some rest.'

They both leave and Robert stops and looks to Valentine, her face betrays her fear and anxiety as he gently grabs her hand and leans forward and whispers in her ear, 'Don't worry. Everything is going to be okay.'

A large fire casts flickering shadows on the cave wall as Chandler stands at attention. Ravanna slowly paces back and forth in front of him, 'Who is leading them?'

Chandler continues staring straight ahead, 'His name is James. He's a Colonel in the Army.

Ravanna stops and turns to him, 'Is he a capable commander?'

Chandler smiles but his eyes remain hard, 'Yes, but he is a mere mortal compared to you my lord.'

Ravanna gives him a curious look, 'And what of the Sheriff who arrived here first? I have a special interest in him.'

Chandler frowns for a moment before quickly regaining his composure, 'He is a separate matter entirely. In fact, I would be more worried about him than the paratroopers.'

Ravanna tilts his head inquisitively, 'Why?'

'I spent some time with him before coming to you and I got to know him. He will want revenge for what has happened to me.'

Ravanna grunts in appreciation, 'Yes, revenge is a powerful sentiment for a warrior to have,' suddenly he turns sharply to Chandler and back hands him. Chandler falls to the ground, his face dripping blood. He tries to stand back up but then Ravanna kicks him in the stomach, 'You are hiding something. How did you manage to resist the Nano machines?' he asks curiously.

Chandler coughs up some blood as Ravanna keeps him pinned to the ground, 'Never mind, I have ways of getting what I want.'

Chandler gasps for breath as Ravanna reaches down with a hand and sprays his viscous, black Nano spray once again into his face. Ravanna waits for a moment as the Nano machines enter Chandler's brain, 'So the Sheriff has a family.'

Chandler looks up at Ravanna in horror as Ravanna looks down at him triumphantly, 'And they are hiding in the observatory. Now that is interesting.'

Chandler glares up at him for a moment but Ravanna knocks him unconscious. Ravanna turns to one of his men, 'I have known this one for a long time. He will never be a true believer. Clean him up and send him back to his friends. We may yet find a use for him.'

Robert, Reese and Tommy sit huddled by a wall with some soldiers; Robert turns and yells 'Fire in the hole!

In turn Reese echoes him, 'Fire in the hole!' A paratrooper engineer presses a button on a detonator and then the wall on the other side of the road explodes.

Above the ringing in their ears Tommy yells, 'Stay down! Wait for the vertical frag!' They stay down as the smoke clears but then they hear a whistling sound as the broken pieces of the wall plop down around them. Robert waits for it to stop and then peers over their cover but most of the wall is still standing. Reese pokes his head up and then looks to Tommy as he laughs, 'Holy hell I can't believe that didn't do anything.'

'Looks like we're going to need a bigger charge,' Reese mutters.

Robert looks to the engineer, 'Get another charge set,' he orders.

The man nods and then sets about priming the charge but then Colonel James walks up with his command team, 'Hey Sheriff, I'll take care of this. I want you and your squad to clear the neighborhood to the south.'

Robert looks up at him annoyed, 'Roger.'

Reese follows Robert and Tommy down a length of wall running along the road in front of the police station but then they come to a hole cut into the concrete. Tommy stops and examines it, 'Firing point.' Reese nods and then sprays it with a neon spray paint but then he looks to Robert, 'Everyone is saying that you saw the commander, I mean Chandler, die in that cave.'

Tommy looks at him with a jolt of surprise but for once he holds his tongue. Robert gives Reese a piercing look before nodding and looking down solemnly.

Reese also looks down awkwardly as he continues, 'Are you sure?'

'As far as I could tell that's what happened,' Robert answers grimly as he places a hand on the young man's shoulder, 'come on, we got work to do.'

Reese gives him a nod and continues down the road but Robert frowns to himself, wondering why the kid has been obsessed with Chandler since they first met. Tommy watches the boy before turning to Robert, 'Either that boy's a no hoper or he's a lation of the commander.'

'Come again?' Robert asks absentmindedly as he turns to his tall friend.

'I said that boy is related to Chandler. He's gotta be,' Tommy says confidently, 'That's the only reason I can think of that explains his odd behavior.'

'Yeah, you might be on to something. But don't ask him. If it is true then Chandler's death would be that much harder on him,' Chandler answers thoughtfully.

'Yeah, yeah, I'm no ocker,' Tommy says as he starts walking after Reese.

Robert looks at him in confusion for a moment before following, 'What?'

They continue on their way but then they hear a voice calling for them from one of the houses. They make their way over and enter but they find a paratrooper standing over a hole cut into the floor. He looks up at them.

'Tunnel', he states gruffly.

Robert peers down into the hole, 'Have you checked it out yet?'

The paratrooper wipes the sweat from his face, 'Could be booby-trapped.'

Reese and Robert look at him with concern but Tommy immediately jumps into the tunnel. He quickly shines his flash light around but it is empty. Robert stares down at him in surprise but then Tommy calls up to them, 'Get down here ya bludgers. It's safe yeah?'

Robert looks to the soldier worriedly, 'Stay here and watch our asses.'

The paratrooper nods in relief as Robert jumps in and Reese follows. Robert shines his flashlight further into the tunnel but all he can see is Tommy's backside as he follows the tunnel's course.

'Come on Robbie, keep up mate,' Tommy calls out softly.

They follow the contours of the tunnel for about 15 meters but then they hear the dull rumble of machinery. They continue but then they see a light at the end of the tunnel. They reach the end and clear but they find a huge subterranean generator, 'What is that?' Reese asks softly.

Robert walks forward, tilting his head to the side, 'It's an atmosphere generator.'

Tommy follows him, 'But isn't this planet's atmosphere already finished?'

'Yeah,' Robert responds distantly.

Tommy stops and stares at him, an inquisitive look on his face, 'So then why the bloody hell did they turn them on?' Robert looks at the immense machine and frowns but he doesn't answer.

Later that night Robert suddenly wakes up and finds that it is completely dark outside. Looking around the small office room in the police station he sees the dark sleeping forms of Tommy and Reese huddled on the floor. Tommy suddenly starts mumbling in his sleep, 'Wankers, you're all wankers!'

Robert smiles groggily as he quietly tip toes out of the room and heads outside to relieve himself. He ambles down the hallway and out into the courtyard of the city hall where the paratroopers have set up a tented command post. Red tactical lighting shines out from the flapped entrance of the tent as Robert walks by but then he over hears someone talking, 'Yes, sir. Our spotters have just confirmed it.'

Suddenly Robert hears Colonel James' deep husky voice, 'So then Ravanna's decided to make this fight lunar.'

'It appears so sir,' the other voice responds.

'Do we have any ships we can use to counter him?' the colonel asks.

'That's a negative colonel,' his subordinate responds dryly.

Colonel James frowns in consternation as he looks down at a map of the colony, 'What could he be planning? We have to try and salvage one of those sabotaged ships on the landing field then.'

'Actually that won't be necessary colonel,' a voice behind him says calmly.

Turning around the colonel is surprised to see Robert standing in the entrance to the tent, 'So you have a ship we could use sheriff?'

'Yes sir,' Robert says confidently, 'I just have one request in exchange for the use of my ship.'

The colonel looks at him expectantly.

'I want to be the one to go up there,' Robert says as his face suddenly becomes grim, 'I owe Ravanna a little payback sir.'

As the two white moons cross the sky overhead Robert straps himself into the cockpit of the Athens and to his surprise finds that all of the instruments are working properly, 'I was almost sure Ravanna's goons would've sabotaged it in some way.' He looks down through the viewport at the paratroopers pulling security out in the forest and gives them a thumbs up to let them know he was ready to go. The paratrooper sergeant in charge nods at him in return and Robert turns the ship on, 'Computer, set a course for the outermost moon.'

Robert looks out through the viewport of the Athens at the slowly approaching moons hanging peacefully ahead of him.

Suddenly visions of Chandler falling to the ground and the accompanying feelings of helplessness begin to stir in his heart. His eyes narrow as his helplessness turns to frustration and then finally to a red hot anger. The grey surface of the moon now fills the viewport and Robert can finally see the lone building of the New Port colony's moon base and next to it a small spacecraft. 'That's Chandler's ship,' he suddenly realizes, 'whoever came up here is alone, just like me.' Then the computer jolts him out of his reverie, 'Prepare for extra atmospheric debarkation.' With a deep breath Robert looks out at the ship before turning and walking back to the ship's airlock.

Robert waits, strapped inside a rather large and cumbersome space suit as the ship's computer slowly circles and then lands. The airlock depressurizes and then the hatch falls to the ground. Immediately all of the air gets sucked out into the vacuum of space. Apart from the sound of his breathing being processed by the suit's air tank everything is completely silent and still. He takes a few hesitant steps outside onto the moon's surface and finds a grey, barren wasteland. Turning to his left he looks down on the cloud covered world below. 'Val,' he thinks to himself as he watches the darkened planet peacefully spinning below. Then he turns to the right and see's the dark grey door of the moon base. He slowly walks over to the entrance and engages the door's unlocking mechanism. It silently opens and Robert ambles in as he fights against the lack of gravity. Turning on the flashlight attached to his suit he finds a long deserted hallway stretching out into the darkness before him. His heart begins to slowly beat harder as he realizes that somewhere in that deep darkness is an enemy. 'But where?' he wonders as he un-holsters his pistol. Robert slowly moves forward into the darkness, his every sense on alert as he leaves the outside world behind and falls deeper into the corrugated steel world surrounding him. He turns around and looks back at the entrance but it is merely a small point of light in the distance. Turning back around he continues into the darkness until it seems to wrap itself around him, pervading his very mind in its unwholesome blackness. Suddenly he hears a voice call out indistinctly from somewhere ahead in the inky shadow, 'Hello?' it says in a childlike voice.

Robert frowns to himself, 'How can there be sound in this vacuum?'

'Where are you?' the voice calls out once again.

'That is definitely a voice,' Robert realizes as he quickens his pace and hurries forward into the darkness.

'Where are you Robert?' the voice asks again plaintively, 'We need your help.'

Robert attempts to run forward in the low gravity atmosphere, 'Is this real?' he wonders worriedly as his heart begins to pound in his chest and sweat beads on his forehead and then drips down his face into his eyes.

He blinks profusely as the voice continues, 'Help us Robert,' it says but now it seems to echo from every direction in a chorus of child-like voices. His space helmet fogs up as he breathes heavily. Dashing forward into the darkness, now barely able to see, faces seem to drift in from the darkness around him as he stumbles forward. Some he recognizes and some he does not. Some are alive and some are dead, rotting and decaying with the relentless passage of time and space as their voices join the chorus. Their screams and cries for help rising in pitch and vigor, worming their way furiously into the black matter of his brain.

'Where were you?' they cry.

'Why didn't you save us?' A thousand voices cry from a thousand directions.

'You let us die!' the voice of the child says in a frightened panic.

And then as the agony and pain of it all reaches a fever pitch Robert tears off his helmet and lets the vacuum of space tear into his vulnerable flesh.

'Hey mate wake up,' Tommy says in a low voice as he gently shakes Robert awake, 'You're having a bad dream.'

Robert suddenly returns to consciousness with a deep breath. Glancing around the room in fear he sees Tommy and Reese fully dressed and looking down at him curiously.

'Come on mate, they're debriefing everyone for the up-coming op,' Tommy adds as he joins Reese at the door.

Robert looks at them in confusion for a moment as the eeriness of his dream slowly passes, 'Ok just give me a minute you wanker.'

Light from the twin moons casts an eerie blue aura on the command compound as Robert, Reese and Tommy enter. They find Colonel James standing in front of a group of officers. He looks over at Robert and nods before continuing his briefing. Gesturing to a map of the town and the outlying region James says, 'We have secured the area around the police station and are now in a good defensive position but it's time to think about getting some help here. In order to do that we have to find and destroy the mechanism they are using to jam our transmissions.' He walks over to a model set up on the dirty floor, 'To do that we will split up into three elements and then push through to the cave system discovered by the Sheriff.'

Tommy turns to Robert, 'As if Ravanna won't be expecting that yeah?' he says in a voice loud enough for everyone in the room to hear.

A paratrooper captain with his name, O'Neil, stenciled on his shoulder, glares at him before raising a hand, 'Who do you want leading the elements?'

The Colonel looks to him, 'I want you leading on the right flank. Lieutenant Williams will follow on the left and I'll be with the command team in the reserve element,' he looks to

Robert, 'I want you to lead us in since you're already familiar with the terrain.'

'More like leading us all into the slaughter. Crickey I need a drink,' Tommy says in a low voice.

Robert pretends to ignore him as he nods his ascent. James turns back to his officers 'All elements will assemble at the line of departure tomorrow at 0630 hours.'

'And no radios, runners only,' a voice says next to Robert, 'you never know if Ravanna is listening in on us.'

Robert turns quickly but to his utter shock he finds Chandler standing there grinning at him.

Inside their small but comfortable sleeping quarters Robert, Reese and Tommy sit around Chandler, their faces full of mirth and happiness at their unexpected reunion.

'Alright lads,' Tommy announces, 'before we all go to an early grave tomorrow I think a little celebration is in order.'

'Here, here!' they call out as Tommy nods to Reese. He pulls out his last pack of cigarettes.

Robert smiles but shakes his head, 'Like hell I'm going to put that crap in my body,' he says as he instead pulls out his last cigar, 'I prefer this much finer form of crap.'

He proffers it to Chandler but he also shakes his head, 'I on the other hand prefer my own form of crap,' he says as he retrieves a slender Winslow pipe from inside his jacket.

'Thank god it didn't break,' he says as he happily remembers the President all those years ago.

'You bloody yanks and your crappy jokes,' Tommy says boisterously, 'Right then as you yanks like to say light em if you got em.'

'It's smoke em if you got em!' Reese says laughingly as they pass around the small plasma lighter.

Robert laughs light heartedly for the first time in a long while and looks to Chandler but for some reason he is staring at Reese with a worried look on his aged face.

As their laughing and joking voices rise with the tobacco smoke into the night sky 300 meters away the twin moons rise higher into the night above the forest surrounding the observatory but then a shadow sprints from the cover of the trees. Ravanna reaches the building and looks up. He carefully reaches down and presses a button on each leg. He grunts in pain for a moment but then he suddenly leaps onto the wall and sprints vertically up to the roof.

Valentine sips at a steaming cup of tea as she watches a monitor showing a video feed of the building's interior absentmindedly. She allows herself to relax as she sips at the delicious tea and wonders at the kindness that Robert showed her earlier. 'When this is all over I'm going to tell him about Jamie,' she decides to herself, 'Maybe at least in that sense some good will come out of this.' She switches the screen and watches Jamie sleeping down the hall.

Jamie sleeps contentedly in a small cot set up in the storage room while on the floor next to him the big brown golden retriever Sam lays down with his head on his paws. His ear twitches at a sound too indistinct for any human to hear. Suddenly his eyes snap open and with a low growl he sees a dark ominous shape silently standing in the doorway as it looks down on the sleeping boy. The dog stands up slowly, a line of fur raised along the back of his spine and growls deeply.

Valentine frowns as one by one, all of the screens in front of her go dead. For a moment she sits there wondering what could be happening but then it hits her. The tea cup falls to the ground and shatters as she scrambles out of the chair and sprints down to the bedroom where Jamie is sleeping. Down the hall she hears a terrible crash and a short muffled scream. She bursts into Jamie's room but Sam lays curled on the floor in a growing pool of some dark liquid. Immediately Valentine runs back into the hallway but then she notices that the escape elevator leading to the roof has been jammed open. From within she hears an odd sound of metal scraping. She immediately sticks her head into the elevator shaft but then she feels her skin crawl in horror. As she tries to hold back the tears streaming down her face she sees a black shape jumping up the shaft from wall to wall and screams in horror, 'Jamie!'

CHAPTER 9

SURVIVAL OF THE FITTEST

The first rays of the sun filter down through the trees and morning mist as Robert, Tommy and Reese sit behind a tree peering forward into the dense forest ahead. They strain their eyes to see through the mist but everything is quiet.

'You know this is going to end badly right?' Tommy says gloomily as he scans his sector.

Robert looks over at him, 'How can you be so sure Tommy?' he asks slightly annoyed.

'Call it a hunch,' Tommy responds coolly.

Suddenly a rock lands next to them. Robert looks back but then he sees a paratrooper waving them forward. They look at each other in a silent moment of understanding and then stand up and cross the line of departure. Reese looks to his right and sees Colonel James' element moving off into the misty forest. They come to a small shack but then someone runs up out of the forest on their right. Reese aims at him but Tommy grabs the barrel and lowers it to the ground as they realize it's a paratrooper from Captain O'Neil's group, 'Easy kid. He's one of ours.'

The runner scowls at him and says, 'Yeah, watch where you're aiming that thing.'

Robert gives him a stern look, 'Relax. What do you want?'

The runner jabs a thumb behind him, 'Captain O'Neil wants you to hold here while he clears through some buildings.'

The lead element of O'Neil's platoon reaches a group of one story buildings surrounded by an orchard and line up against the wall outside the door. The platoon sergeant walks up to the compound entrance and peers inside but it is empty.

'Fire in the hole!' he yells as he pulls out a grenade and tosses it in. An explosion rocks the air and dust pours out of the doorway. 'Alright, Greenley on me,' he calls out. Private Greenley moves up and they both enter the compound. The sergeant pushes up through the dust and makes a right turn but then he comes face to face with Ravanna. He lifts up his gun but then him and Greenley are shot from behind.

Robert, Tommy and Reese listen as a huge fire fight rages in the distance. 'See I told you we were screwed on this one,'

Tommy says in frustration, 'my hunches are always right. But no one ever listens to me.'

'Well if you're so sure then why did you even come with us?' Robert asks impatiently, 'You're not a paratrooper or law enforcement.'

'You're wrong there mate,' the tall Australian says in a serious voice but then he smiles, 'I guess there's no harm in telling you now yeah?'

Robert looks to Reese but he just shrugs.

'I wasn't always like this you know,' Tommy says as old memories come flooding back, 'A long time ago I was code name Viper with the Special Operations Command. Ravanna was my officer in command. That's how I know that this is definitely going to end badly my friend.'

He looks up at Robert and for once his face looks worn with old trauma and grief. Suddenly Lieutenant Williams walks up with his command team and startles them. 'Why are you stopped?' he asks impatiently.

'Just got a message from a runner telling us to hold,' Robert says calmly as he looks at the young Lieutenant, 'O'Neil has to clear some buildings.'

Lieutenant Williams gives him a sharp look, 'Well, I just heard from Colonel James and he wants us to move up through the orchard and keep O'Neil from getting flanked. So get moving,' he orders angrily. Robert gives Reese and Tommy a look but Reese just gets up and leads the way forward, 'I'll take point Sheriff,' he says without looking back.

'You ready Viper?' Robert asks Tommy with a grin.

The shadow passes from Tommy's face and he laughs, 'Hell yeah mate. Let's get those bastards, yeah?'

'Yeah,' Robert says as he trudges after Reese. They push through a thicket but then they come to the well-ordered lines of the orchard. Robert turns and makes sure Tommy and the other soldiers are following them before tapping on Reese's shoulder. He nods and they move forward. Suddenly they hear someone speak close by. They both wordlessly sink to a knee and wait but then four armed men, their bodies covered in grass and foliage to camouflage them, walk out in front of them. They both freeze for a moment as the men slowly get nearer but then Reese opens fire, the explosive rounds from the machine gun tearing ragged holes in their flesh and blowing off arms and legs. Their death screams pierce the morning air as Robert turns and says, 'Reese, pull back.' Reese nods but then another group of enemy hiding further back in the orchard open fire on them. High velocity rounds rip through the air all around them. They both turn and Reese unloads on their position. The unseen enemy is forced to take cover as he peppers them with explosive rounds that shake the ground. Robert grabs his shoulder, 'Pull back!' Reese fires another burst as Robert bounds back. Turning to cover Reese in turn, Robert watches as Reese runs over to him but then a spray of blood flies through the air as Reese takes a round through the chest and falls to the ground. Robert ducks behind a tree as the incoming fire intensifies and screams, 'Man down!'

Colonel James stands with Chandler and the headquarters element as they listen to the fighting going on up ahead but then a runner emerges from the trees. The runner, gasping for breath, barely manages to blurt out, 'We got a man down.'

Chandler takes a step forward, 'Who is it?'

'It's the rookie who was with the Sheriff,' the runner says.

'Reese?' Chandler asks a note of panic evident in his voice.

The runner nods in affirmation but Chandler is already running forward toward the sounds of intense shooting ahead.

Chandler runs past the paratroopers taking cover and reaches the orchard but then one of the NCOs grabs him and pulls him down, 'Sir, you'd better stay down.' Chandler suddenly becomes furious and shakes him off, 'We have a man down up there damn it!'

The paratroopers look at Chandler in surprise and shock, 'The incoming's too intense sir!'

Tommy suddenly runs out of the orchard and stands exposed in the midst of the hail of incoming rounds as he looks to the paratroopers lying on the ground around him, 'Right! I want three men on me. Reference green George around the orchard corner, on the high ground to the north, enemy fighters spotted putting enfilading fire on our position.' Seeing him standing exposed the rest of the men immediately follow his example and three of them follow him to the far edge of the orchard.

Chandler looks to the squad leader, 'Lay down covering fire!' he yells at the top of his lungs. All of the paratroopers open fire in a deafening fusillade as Chandler sprints forward. A bullet sings past his head but then he dives down next to Robert. Chandler looks to Reese, 'Is he alright?' he screams above the din.

Robert looks at him in surprise, 'I don't know,' he yells back.

Chandler nods grimly, 'We have to get him out of here. You cover and I'll carry him.'

'Roger,' Robert yells back as he picks up Reese's machine gun. He rolls out from behind the cover of the tree and begins spraying bursts of high explosive rounds. His ears ringing from the explosions, Chandler lifts Reese onto his back and carries him to their line. Robert fires one last burst and stands up to go but then a round suddenly tears through his left arm in a spray of blood.

Robert screams, 'I'm hit! I'm hit!' His voice is high pitched with pain and fear as he stumbles forward into the fire line and falls to the ground. He looks at his arm but a chunk of his flesh is missing. The medic runs up, he kneels next to him and starts bandaging him but Robert pushes him away, 'Take care of Reese first doc.'

The medic shakes his head, 'He's already dead.'

Chandler bends down and examines Reese's unblinking eyes but then Reese suddenly spasms for a moment and looks right at him. 'He's still alive!' Chandler yells earnestly.

The medic looks down at Reese in surprise, 'What? Are you sure?'

'Yeah, he just looked at me. He's still alive!' Chandler yells at him still struggling to be heard above the deafening sounds of battle.

The medic checks his pulse and then opens his eye lid, 'He has a weak pulse. If he's going to make it we have to get him out of here right now.'

Robert stands up on his own strength, 'I'll keep you covered but we have to go now.'

Four of the paratroopers carry Reese on a stretcher while Robert and Chandler walk a few paces ahead of them. Robert looks to Chandler, 'How do you think they knew we were coming?'

Chandler frowns in thought as if suddenly realizing something, 'I think I might have an idea.'

Suddenly Chandler stops. Robert looks up but then his heart skips a beat. Standing in the center of a clearing ahead of them they see Ravanna. He stands quietly, waiting for them to make a move as a cold wind blows through the tall grass around him.

Chandler quickly turns to Robert, his eyes a little wide with fear, 'Get Reese out of here.' He turns back and faces Ravanna, 'I'll keep him off your back.'

The stretcher bearers immediately turn back the way they came to take the long way around to the base but Robert hesitates, 'You should go with them, I'll stay.'

Chandler turns and looks at him but he is no longer afraid, instead Robert notices a fire burning in his eyes, 'No, you have to take care of my son. Now make sure he survives.'

Robert nods as he finally understands, 'He's your son?'

'That's right,' Chandler responds gruffly.

Robert looks at him, still feeling surprised but he refuses to budge, 'Well if he's your son then you need to go with him.'

Chandler suddenly gives him a pained look, 'I can't,' he falters.

Robert gives him an inquisitive look.

'I'm pretty sure he bugged me with Nano-machines,' Chandler finally admits, 'I'm a liability to everyone.'

Robert looks at him intently as Chandler chokes up a little, 'Now I want you to promise me that you will look after Reese for me. I was never a proper father to the boy. This is the least I can do for him. Now go!' he yells as he pulls off his combat pack and throws it to the ground. Robert nods resolutely before turning and running into the forest after Reese. Chandler turns and looks at Ravanna, his eyes glistening in the sunlight, but a new lightness has come over him and for the first time since the destruction of the Earth he feels a certain sense of exhilaration. In giving up all hope he realizes that he has finally found true freedom. He looks at Ravanna but the black garbed man doesn't say anything and just drops a hand down to the small pistol strapped to his thigh. Chandler smirks before nodding and reaching down and placing a hand on his own pistol holster. Slowly they begin to circle each other. For a moment they just stare at each other as the wind blows through the trees but then in the flash of a split second they both draw their pistols and unload in a flurry of gunshots. The shooting suddenly ends as abruptly as it began. Ravanna looks down at his chest and places a hand on the small dents where Chandler's rounds were deflected by his armor plating before looking back up at Chandler lying in the grass. He takes a deep breath underneath his space helmet before slowly walking over. As he approaches Chandler he reloads the small black pistol and primes it. Chandler groans in pain as he looks down at the three bloody spots slowly growing on his chest and stomach. He looks up at Ravanna but there is a gleam in his eye, 'I had a feeling you were wearing armor father.' Ravanna doesn't respond and simply aims his pistol at Chandler's head. 'That's why I got one of these ready,' Chandler continues smiling as he lifts his hand out of the grass clenching a primed grenade. Ravanna looks at him sharply in a moment of panic before he releases the trigger and blows them both up.

CHAPTER 10

The Plan

Robert and Tommy sit by Reese in an ad hoc medic's station set up in the police station. The men sit quietly as they listen to the sound of the rain pouring outside. Robert sighs as he watches Reese slowly breathe in and out.

'So he was Chandler's son?' Tommy says as he looks to Robert.

'Yeah, I don't know how I'm going to tell him about what happened,' Robert says with a grimace.

'That is if he even pulls through,' Tommy says mournfully.

The medic walks up, his uniform covered in blood from treating all the casualties of the day's fighting. Robert looks up at him, 'How is he doing?'

The medic bends down and examines Reese, 'He should be stabilized, for now.'

'How long can we keep him like this doc?' Tommy asks as he looks back down at the unconscious young man.

'He needs a doctor,' the medic sighs as he closes his tired eyes and rubs his temples, 'the battalion surgeon got hit on the first night and there's only so much I can do.' Robert nods and looks down at Reese with concern. The medic opens his eyes and glances down at Robert, 'You should let me look at that wound sheriff.' Robert nods absentmindedly as the medic pulls off the bandage. He frowns as he examines the bloody gouge torn through Robert's shoulder muscle. Robert winces with pain as he probes the wound. The medic turns and opens his medical kit, 'I don't think there's much I can do here. All I can do is put on a fresh field dressing for now.'

'Just do it slowly,' Robert says gingerly as he stifles a groan.

The medic unwraps a new dressing and places it on the wound, 'You know, we have some booze for the pain if you want it?' the medic adds with a raised eyebrow.

Robert looks up at Tommy but then he shakes his head, 'No thanks doc, we're clean these days.'

Tommy smiles gratefully; 'Yeah, we don't need that tosh in our systems no more,' but then his smile vanishes as he looks up at the door. Robert follows his gaze but then he sees Valentine standing in the doorway dripping wet from the rain, her face puffy from crying.

Robert looks at her in surprise, 'Val?' but she doesn't respond and hugs him tightly. He winces in pain as she brushes past his wound.

'What is it?' he asks as he looks at her in concern, 'Where's Jamie?'

'He's been taken,' she manages to blurt out as the tears begin to swell in her eyes again, 'Oh Robert, I don't know what to do.'

Robert grabs her hand as he looks into her shining blue eyes, 'I'll think of something. Don't worry. I'll get him back. I promise.' Suddenly Robert's backpack radio comes to life. He turns on the speaker but then the cold, familiar metallic voice of Ravanna comes on the line, 'I am Ravanna, the redeemer of mankind.'

'Looks like he finally unblocked the signal jammer,' Tommy says as he frowns at the radio, 'lot of damn good the mission today did,' he adds bitterly.

'I have broken our radio silence to inform you that the entire 3rd Space fleet is en route and will be here within the next two hours,' Ravanna states coldly. Robert and Valentine exchange a look of surprise. 'However, I assure you that we will have an adequately sized response. I know you will enjoy it thoroughly,' the evil sounding voice says brusquely and then signs off.

Valentine looks at Robert and Tommy in confusion, 'I wonder what he meant by that.'

Tommy looks to Robert but he is deep in thought, 'Are you thinking what I'm thinking mate?'

Robert nods as he looks down at Reese and then it suddenly all comes together. He turns to Valentine, 'I think I know what he's planning,' he says clearly and confidently, 'Stay here and take care of this soldier. I promised his father I would keep him alive.' He turns to go with Tommy but Valentine calls after him in confusion, 'Where are you guys going?'

Robert turns back to her and looks at her keenly, 'I have to check something out.'

Robert and Tommy walk into the paratrooper's headquarters but find only chaos. Colonel James sits behind a large oak desk but he is being swamped by radio calls from scattered paratrooper units now that the signal jammer has been disabled. He looks up at Robert and the towering Australian but he doesn't try to hide his irritation, 'What is it Sheriff?'

'Sir, we think we know what Ravanna might be up to,' Robert says excitedly.

James looks up at him unimpressed, 'Elaborate.'

Robert nods and continues, 'When I first got here I listened to some recordings made by a detective. The only clue he ever found was that the victims had been attacked with an aerosol based weapon.'

Colonel James frowns, 'And what does that have to do with our current situation?'

'Later on Tommy and I discovered a tunnel that had been dug by the enemy but for some reason it led into one of the atmospheric generators,' Robert continues quickly.

'You had better sum this all up pretty fast,' Colonel James demands impatiently.

Tommy looks down at the Colonel angrily but then Robert places a restraining hand on his arm before turning back to James, 'Colonel, the generator had been turned on when we arrived even though they finished terraforming years ago. We believe that Ravanna is planning to use the atmospheric generators to launch a massive chemical attack on the fleet when they arrive.'

Colonel James gives him a piercing look for a moment as he makes his decision but then his eyes seem to soften, 'What do you two need to stop him?'

Robert and Tommy lead a platoon of dirty but resolute looking paratroopers through the dark streets as the double moons slowly rise into the clear night sky. They stealthily walk along the neighborhood streets they had cleared the day before until they finally arrive at the house where they found the tunnel. Robert leads the way inside but the darkened house is empty. Jumping down into the tunnel he quickly scans for any sort of threat but there is no discernible sign of the enemy. He motions for Tommy to follow. As the paratroopers jump down behind them one by one Robert leads the way down the darkened confines of the tunnel. He makes it about halfway but then he suddenly spots a gleam in the darkness. Peering forward carefully he can barely make out a trip wire blocking the tunnel in front of him.

'Trip wire,' he whispers to Tommy.

'Right,' Tommy whispers nervously as he quickly lifts a fist and signals for the men to stop. He shines a small flash light forward to help Robert as he bends down to examine the trap.

'It looks like a simple trip wire setup,' Tommy whispers to Robert, 'Follow the wire to the detonator and then jam it in place so you can cut the wire yeah?'

'Yeah,' Robert whispers back nervously.

Following the silver thread of the trip wire stretching from one side of the tunnel to the other Robert finds the detonator attached to the opposite wall just like Tommy said. Pulling out his knife Robert holds his breath as he carefully uses the blade to jam the detonator into place.

'Easy now mate, nice and slow,' Tommy whispers to him soothingly.

As sweat drips from his forehead Robert pulls out his pliers and then, hands shaking from the adrenaline he reaches forward and snips the wire, half expecting a detonation but nothing happens. He sighs in relief as Tommy turns to the men and gives them the thumbs up.

'You ready?' Tommy whispers forward to Robert but then they feel something shift below them. Looking down Tommy suddenly realizes what happened, 'Secondary!' he yells as the ceiling above him splits and then cracks. Diving forward, Robert barely makes it as the tunnel collapses behind him with a crash. The tunnel fills with dust from the avalanche of stone but he is unscathed. Coughing, Robert turns to the rubble and calls out, 'Tommy! Can you hear me?' He listens for a response but then he hears a dull rumble emanating from above as dust starts to sprinkle down on him. His heart pounds in his chest as Robert sprints forward, the tunnel completely collapsing behind him. Screaming in fear and tension he gathers all his strength for one last superhuman effort and hurtles himself forward into the generator room as a cloud of dust explodes behind him. Coughing incessantly and blinded from the bright ceiling lights, Robert stumbles forward. His eyes finally adjust but then he realizes that he isn't alone. Looking up he sees about fifty men aiming assault rifles at him. And then Ravanna, his helmet and space suit severely damaged, walks out of another tunnel with Jamie.

A dust covered Tommy, blood streaming from a gash on his forehead, suddenly runs into the medic station but he finds Valentine and the medic sitting with a now conscious Reese. She looks up at him in surprise but he turns to the medic, 'Hey doc we need ya right now.'

'What happened?' the medic asks as he picks up his team medic pack.

Tommy presses a field dressing to his head wound, 'The bloody tunnel collapsed on our guys.'

Reese suddenly looks at him, 'The tunnel leading to the generator room?'

Valentine looks down at him inquisitively, 'Generator room?'

'Yeah,' Reese says, 'we found out that the enemy is using the planet's atmospheric generators for something.'

Tommy nods gravely, 'They booby-trapped the tunnel leading to it and now there's nothing we can do to stop Ravanna from using the generators to release a chemical attack on the fleet coming in.'

Valentine frowns in concentration, 'Maybe there is something we can do,' she says in a thoughtful voice.

The men all look at her in confusion.

Valentine suddenly seems to become aware of them and blurts out, 'EMP. You guys have nukes right?' Without waiting for a response she continues, 'If we create an electromagnetic pulse in the atmosphere it would shut down the electronics used to power the generators so that Ravanna wouldn't be able to use them.'

'Yeah but that would also knock out all of our equipment too,' Tommy says as he mulls it over.

'At the moment it's really our only choice,' Valentine says sternly.

CHAPTER 11

THE MAN IN THE MASK

Robert stands with his hands in the air, his weapon strapped to his back, 'Sheriff Robert!' Jamie says hopefully.

Robert gives him an encouraging look but Ravanna just laughs coldly, 'I don't think he's in any position to help you boy.'

Robert looks at Ravanna and Jamie but then something catches his eye. Behind them, two of Ravanna's men are carrying a large glass container filled with a viscous black vapor.

'So, you must be the Sheriff. I've heard a lot about you from your friends and family,' Ravanna says as he places a black hand on Jamie's shoulder, 'Now then, if you value the life of this boy, place your weapon on the ground.' Robert lifts his gun up over his head but they all cover him tightly. He slowly places it on the ground. Within his black space helmet

Ravanna chuckles softly, 'Good choice,' he takes a step forward as one of his men grabs hold of Jamie, 'Now then, I have a surprise for you. Something I've been wanting to show you since you first arrived.' Reaching up slowly he twists his helmet slightly to the left and then lifts it from his head. Robert feels a shiver run up his spine as he looks into Ravanna's face, a powerful sense of horror turns his stomach ice cold as he stares into a mirror reflection of his own face, although much older and decayed, looking back at him. Jamie looks up at him, eyes bulging in fear and confusion. Ravanna grins malevolently at their reactions.

'How is this possible?' Robert asks in shock.

Ravanna's smile broadens, 'It's quite simple. You are one of my clones,' suddenly his smile disappears, 'Now you know what I felt all those years ago when I too had to experience the horror of knowing that you are not special or unique but merely a pawn for the government.'

Robert frowns as he thinks back on everything in his life, 'How?' he wonders. It had all seemed so real. He looks up at Ravanna, 'When was this done to me?'

'No one on Earth wanted to go live out on third rate colony worlds,' Ravanna says as he pulls his pistol from its harness, 'Why would anyone want to leave the comfort and perfection that the Earth had become? So the all wise and all powerful United Nations began a cloning program to ensure that the Earth was well supplied by her slaves on the colonies.'

Robert nods grimly, finally understanding.

'What right did they have to do such a thing?' Ravanna asks impassionedly.

One of Ravanna's men steps forward and Ravanna nods, 'It is nearly time to welcome our visitors.'

He lifts his pistol and aims at Robert, 'I know you would never join us in taking revenge. Just like Chandler.' He slowly squeezes the trigger but then they hear a muffled boom come from outside followed by a heavy shock wave that shakes the ground.

Valentine, Tommy and Colonel James shield their eyes as the massive white corona of a nuclear blast rips across the atmosphere.

'That is just ripper,' Tommy says as the blast diminishes and they look up spellbound. Within a few seconds all of the lights, radios and sophisticated targeting equipment used by the paratroopers go dead.

James looks to Valentine, 'This better work,' he says threateningly but she doesn't seem to hear him as she finally looks up at the now blue nuclear halo.

Surges of electricity run up and down Ravanna's body. He starts to violently shake and falls to the concrete floor as the generator suddenly explodes and knocks out his men. Robert gets up and sprints over to Jamie, 'You okay?'

Jamie nods fearfully, 'Yeah.'

Robert glances around the room and spots the exit, 'Come on. Let's get out of here.' Lifting the young boy to his feet he rushes him out the door. Behind them amid the smoke and fire Ravanna regains control of himself and staggers to his feet. Smiling bitterly, he pulls out a charge handle and presses the button.

The massive Navy Space Carrier filled with marines approaches the cloud covered planet of Wolf 359 but then overhead the twin moons are suddenly consumed by massive explosions.

Valentine sees Colonel James run into the command room, 'What's happening?' she asks fearfully as the very ground trembles from the force of the explosions.

'Ravanna's done it again,' Colonel James says in a panicked voice, 'The moons are breaking up. I've contacted the carrier and they're going to pick us up but we have to leave now.'

'How the hell did he manage that?' Tommy asks in dismay.

Valentine ignores him and looks to the colonel, 'What about Robert and Jamie?'

James gives her a grim look, 'They're cut off.' He turns to one of his staff, 'Begin the evacuation,' he orders as he turns away.

But Valentine refuses to be deterred, 'Well we have to rescue them!'

'Yeah, that's my mate out there!' Tommy adds angrily.

Colonel James turns back once more, his face suddenly drawn and tired, 'I'm sorry but if they don't make it to us then we have to leave without them.'

CHAPTER 12

THE FINAL COUNTDOWN

Robert and Jamie follow the generator service tunnel but then they hear Ravanna laugh somewhere behind them. Picking up the pace they come to a ladder leading up to a hatch. As he glances behind them Robert says, 'You go first Jamie.' Jamie climbs up as fast as he can, pushes open the hatch and pulls himself out. He suddenly finds himself outside in a field surrounded by tall pines but then he sees the moons breaking up over head. Robert climbs out of the hatch next but then he nearly falls back inside as Ravanna grabs his foot from below.

Colonel James stands with Valentine and Tommy outside the shuttle as they load up with the paratroopers, 'He's not going to make it,' James states sternly as he looks at Valentine.

Turning to him angrily she says, 'They will make it. Just give them one more minute.'

The Colonel shakes his head as he glances up at the destroyed moons, 'No, we have to leave now.' He gestures to two marines to take her aboard.

'No!' Valentine screams, 'I'm not leaving without my son and husband!' She tries her hardest to resist but a marine medic walks up from behind and sedates her.

'Get her on the shuttle,' James commands, his face hard.

'Oi!' Tommy shouts angrily, 'that was uncalled for mate. Now you gone and made me do my lolly you twat.' The marine's look at one another slightly confused but then Tommy crashes into them full force.

Jamie watches in stunned silence as Robert and Ravanna fight with everything they have. Robert knocks Ravanna down but then he sees that the Athens is in the next field. Robert calls out, 'Jamie! Get to my ship!'

'I see it!' Jamie calls back. Robert and Jamie make a run for it but then the planet's gravity starts to slow down as the moons break up. First just debris and twigs start to rise into the air but then rocks and heavier branches begin to slowly lose their purchase on the ground. Robert and Jamie start to run like they are on the moon but then Ravanna leaps forward and tackles Robert. Robert yells in frustration as Ravanna gets him in a hold.

'Run Jamie! Get out of here!' Robert screams as he struggles to break free.

Ravanna whispers into his ear, 'You are going to die. Are you ready?' Robert watches as Jamie makes it to the ship and boards safely. He tries to free his arms but then he feels Ravanna's dagger strapped to his leg. He attempts to grab it but he can't hold on. Then the first lunar fragments begin to land all around them. They both look up and see a huge rock hurtling right toward them. Robert tries to push away but Ravanna holds him in place as he watches it approach. Ravanna whispers, 'Accept it.' The rock hurtles toward them at an increasing speed but then Robert's fingers find a grip on the dagger. He quickly unsheathes it and stabs Ravanna in the thigh. Pushing himself out of the way he manages to dive away just as the rock lands right on top of Ravanna.

Taking one last look back in shock and distress Robert turns and runs as fast as he can but the gravity keeps slowing down. Using all of his strength to fight against the lack of gravity he finally makes it to his ship. He seals the deck and returns to normal gravity. Sprinting up to the bridge, he finds Jamie strapped in.

'Sheriff Robert!' Jamie exclaims in relief.

'Don't worry. We're okay Jamie,' Robert responds reassuringly. Suddenly the lunar break up intensifies outside. Robert starts the computer but it doesn't respond. 'Computer?' he asks in consternation. The machine whirs for a moment but then the screen flashes a message.

'Manual restart required,' the computer responds calmly.

Robert suddenly remembers the EMP blast that saved him from Ravanna also shut down every electronic device. He sprints to the maintenance room as his heart pounds in his chest and throws open the computer server. It is a mess of wires and pipes. 'I need you now Val,' he mutters to himself. Suddenly a piece of the moon the size of a cruise ship lands right on top of the colony and completely obliterates it.

'Hurry Sheriff!' Jamie calls from the cockpit. The ship shakes from the concussion but then Robert sees a charging pump with the words "Manual Restart" written above it.

Grabbing the handle, he pumps it up and then presses the restart button. The computer whirs to life for a moment but then it stalls.

Robert curses in fear and anger as he grabs the handle again and pumps it up even more this time.

'Come on! Work!' he yells as he presses the restart button again. The computer whirs to life again but this time it stays on. He runs back up to the cockpit and straps himself in. 'Computer, switch over to manual flight controls,' he orders breathlessly. Grabbing the joystick, he pulls it back towards him and the ship rises into the night sky. But then, just as he begins to feel a semblance of hope it quickly fades away as they see a virtual hail storm of lunar debris streaming through the planet's atmosphere and coming right for them. Jamie gasps in fear as they fly head on into the tempest. A multitude of small fragments suddenly pepper the viewport, cracking it dangerously. Robert turns the ship out of the storm but into the path of an enormous boulder sized rock. Inverting the ship, he barely manages to dodge it at the last moment but with a terrible screech the top of the ship grazes the uneven surface of the rock. And with that they finally make it into orbit just as the planet explodes in a blinding flash behind them. Breathing a sigh of relief Robert throttles down the engine.

'Is it finally over Robert?' Jamie asks fearfully.

Robert says, 'Yeah, I think so,' he looks around as he tries to process everything that's happened. Settling back down into the command chair he gives Jamie a reassuring smile but Jamie is staring in horror at something. Following his gaze Robert suddenly notices that the terminal velocity of the Athen's engines is causing the cracks on the viewport glass to slowly spread across its face.

'It's breaking!' Jamie screams in panic as tears stream down his face. He covers his eyes in terror as Robert tries to slow down but the differential causes the ship to shake and the cracks to get even worse. As the ship slows down Robert and Jamie watch in agony as the cracks spread further and further. Just when it looks like the window is about to finally shatter the ship comes to a halt and the cracking finally stops.

Sweat drips from his brow as Robert finally collapses from the exertion and slumps down into the chair. In the distance Jamie sees the massive frame of the Space Carrier turn and head over in their direction.

EPILOGUE

A New Life

The battered sheriff patrol ship touches down inside the huge navy carrier. The ramp descends and Robert and Jamie walk down into the cold brightness of the ship but then they see Valentine standing across the hangar. Jamie runs over to his mother and hugs her, 'Jamie!' she exclaims in relief, 'I was so scared I wouldn't see you again. Are you hurt?'

Jamie looks up at her smiling, 'Don't worry mom, I'm okay. I had Sheriff Robert to protect me.'

'Game as Ned Kelly if I might be so bold to say my man,' a familiar Australian accented voice says from behind Robert. He turns and finds Tommy smiling at him.

Robert smiles uncertainly, 'Uh yeah mate good to see you too.'

Tommy turns and looks over at Valentine, 'Looks like you got yourself a right ripper little family over there.'

'Well it's not exactly my family,' Robert says as he glances over at them.

'Oh I don't know mate. I got a hunch that you might find out otherwise yeah?' He says with a nod.

Robert looks at him for a moment before smiling incredulously, 'Yeah mate.'

'Good on ya, now make me proud and don't muck it up ya lousy mug,' he says with a smile. Robert smiles back before turning and walking toward Valentine and Jamie. She gives Robert a look of profound gratitude as she holds Jamie in her arms but then Robert sees the medic attending to Reese as he lays on a gurney. Robert suddenly turns and walks up to Reese. The medic nods to him as he moves on to the other casualties. Reese looks up at Robert but he has trouble focusing his eyes, 'I keep asking about my father but no one seems to know where he is.'

Robert looks down for a moment before looking back up at the young man's expectant face.

'He didn't make it,' Reese says forlornly, 'I guess I knew it deep down inside.'

Robert looks up at him fiercely, 'Reese, you have no idea how much he cared about you. When you got hit he ran up through some of the most intense fire to save you. And then when Ravanna showed up he sacrificed his life to make sure we could get you to the aid station.'

'Really?' Reese asks in surprise, his face brightening as Robert places a reassuring hand on his shoulder and nods.

'Thank you,' Reese says, sounding stronger now. He looks over at Valentine, 'I think she's waiting for you over there,' he says with a grin. Robert gives him a smile before turning and walking over to Valentine and Jamie.

'You guys doing ok?' he asks as he ruffles Jamie's long brown hair.

'Yeah,' Jamie says gratefully.

Robert looks up at Valentine but she is smiling sweetly at him, 'Jamie, remember what I told you about your father?'

Jamie looks up at her inquisitively.

'Well,' Valentine says as she looks down at her son, 'This is your father,' she says as silent tears of joy and relief begin to stream down her cheeks. Robert looks deeply into her shining blue eyes before gently reaching down and grabbing her hand.